I0763419

HE'S MY SON'S BEST FRIEND.
BUT IT'S NOT WHAT YOU THINK...

WHAT IF IT'S RIGHT?

A SHILOH SPRINGS LOVE STORY

JB HELLER

Published by- Author JB Heller

Cover Design by- JeBDesigns

Editing by- Jenn Lockwood Editing

Formatted by – JeBDesigns

Prologue

Weston

She releases a strangled groan, "Weston."

My name on her lips, that soft breathy moan does something to my rational thoughts. I close the distance between our mouths and do all the things I've been aching to do to those lips.

Tory's hands slide up into my hair as she clings to me, and I pull away just a whisper. "Don't make me keep waiting, Tory," I breathe.

She shudders under my palms, then she closes her eyes so tight her nose crinkles. "Weston, this is so wrong."

Smoothing my thumb over her lips again, her eyes flash open, and I grin at her. "But what if it's right?"

Chapter One

Victoria

Fourteen Years Ago...

I can't wipe the grin off my face as the wind whips through my hair, sending it flying around me. My stomach dips and lurches, but my smile grows wider. I glance at my eight-year-old nephew, Finn, clutching the safety bar locked in around his chest for dear life. But his smile is just as wide as mine.

"Woo!" he screams out in joy, and I join him as the rollercoaster takes its final dive.

When it comes to a stop, I help him out of his seat, his little legs wobbling under him.

"That was so cool! Can we do it again?" he begs, his big brown eyes melting my heart.

"Hell yeah, we can. But we better check on your mom first. She's probably having heart palpitations right now. We better go let her know you survived," I laugh.

Finn rolls his eyes. "She's such a chicken."

I ruffle his hair, grinning down at him. "I know, but that's what you've got me for. To do all the cool stuff with you," I say with a wink then take his hand as we exit the ride and find my sister at the gate, waiting for us.

Her hands are clenched around the railing so tight her knuckles are white. When she catches sight of us, she releases a relieved sigh and clutches a hand over her heart. "Oh my God! You are never going on a death trap like that again! I can't believe I let you talk me into letting Finn go on that thing," she rants, pulling Finn into her arms as she speaks.

It's my turn to roll my eyes. "Chill out, Jacq, let the kid live a little. Look at him; he's fine."

Finn lifts his head and looks up into her eyes. "It was so awesome, Mom. Can I go again? Pleease!"

Jacq smiles down at her son and sighs. "I'm sure it was awesome, but there is no way you are going on that thing again. Not today, anyway. My heart just about jumped right out of my chest."

"But Mom..." Finn whines.

She shakes her head. "Maybe next year. Let's go ride the dodge 'em cars!"

Finn's face lights up, and he nods eagerly before taking off in the direction of the next ride. Jacq and I follow him closely, our arms linked at the elbow. "How can you say no to that face?" I ask her.

She laughs at me. "Just wait until you have kids, Tory."

"Dude, no. I'm eighteen, that's not going to happen. Not now, not ever." I cringe at the mere thought.

We buy our tickets then race each other to get to the nearest car. When the buzzer sounds, I ram straight into the side of Finn, sending his blue car into a spin until he's facing me. His wicked little smile lights up, and he wastes no time coming back at me.

Laughter bubbles from me like a madwoman. Jacq even gets in on the action too, and I lose count of the number of times her purple car rams my silver one. I love my sister, and as uptight as she can sometimes be, she knows how to let go and have fun too.

The rest of the day flies by with hot dogs, laughter, and way too much candy.

Finn's practically comatose on the drive home, flopped back in his seat, his little hands clutching his tummy. "Ughh, my tummy hurts," he mumbles.

"I told you to stop eating, but no, you didn't listen to me. You did this to yourself, Finn," my sister scolds.

"I know, I know. I'm a rebel. I can't help it, Mom," Finn whines back.

I cover my mouth to stop my laughter, and Jacq sends me a sidelong glare. I shrug her off. "The kid's hilarious; it's not my fault."

Jacq rolls her eyes but doesn't say anything else.

It is just about dusk, and after spending the whole day at the carnival, we're all exhausted. My eyes flutter closed as I lay my head back on my headrest and promptly fall asleep.

The next thing I know, my head is tossed to the side, smacking against the window with such force the glass smashes.

I try to gain my bearings, but everything's blurry and spinning out of control. Blinking rapidly, I wipe at my eyes, a distraught scream ripping from my throat as my vision finally clears and Jacq's body comes into view. She's hanging limply at an odd angle, blood covering her beautiful face.

"Jacq," I shriek. "Jacq, wake up!"

A groan filters through the static filling my ears. It's coming from the backseat. *Oh God, Finn.* I try to turn around to see him, but my arm is pinned, restricting my movement. "Finn, buddy, you okay?" I call to him.

"Tory," he cries. "Mommy isn't moving. Why isn't Mommy moving?" Then, he screams for her, "Mommy!"

"She's okay, buddy; we're going to be okay," I croak, my voice shaking with the exertion it takes to speak. My chest constricts as the words pass my lips.

It's the biggest lie I have ever told.

JACQ HIT AN OIL SLICK ON THE ROAD, CAUSING THE CAR TO SPIN out of control and collide with oncoming traffic. Her side took the brunt of the impact, killing her instantly.

Finn escaped with a few scratches from the broken glass and a broken wrist.

My arm was so badly damaged it took a handful of pins and bolts to put it back together.

The emotional scars from that day would haunt us long after our bones mended, and our skin healed.

Chapter Two

Victoria

Thirteen Years Ago . . .

"Finn, I'm not arguing with you about this. You have to go to school!" I'm raising my voice. I really don't like raising my voice at him, but he's pushing my buttons this morning.

"No!" he yells back. "Everyone looks at me weird; I hate it."

Sighing, I sit down at the table and push my fingers into my hair. I'm only nineteen; I am not equipped to raise a nine-year-old kid. I'm still practically one myself. "Why do you think they look at you weird, Finn?" I ask, trying to keep the exasperation from my tone.

He flops back into his chair across from mine, folding his arms over his chest as he averts his gaze. "Because I don't have a mom anymore," he whispers.

The pain in his voice pierces my heart, and I struggle to keep my composure in front of him. "Finn, buddy, you will always have your mom. She just lives in our hearts now." I watch as he fights back his tears. It isn't fair that he had to go through this.

He clenches his little fists then slams them on the table. "I don't want her in my heart! I want her here!" he yells, shoving from the table. He disappears down the hall, his door slamming shut moments later.

As soon as I hear his lock engage, I break down. He won't be coming out of there today. And I won't be going to work.

I press my forehead to the table, a sob lodged in my throat. "I know you thought I could do this, Jacq, but I can't. I can't replace you," I murmur quietly to my dead sister. "Please, just send me a sign, anything to help me make sense of it all. Why did you think I could do this?"

Finn's father died a week after his second birthday in an oil rig explosion. Jacq had been devastated, but having Finn helped her heal.

I get up, run my hand through my hair, and head to the bathroom to wash my tear-stained face. Looking at my reflection, I don't see a nineteen-year-old girl with her whole life ahead of her. No, I see a sad, unsure girl who hopes like hell she's making the right choices—since now all my decisions affect not only myself, but more importantly, Finn.

I scrub my hands down my face again before drying it off and heading out to call my boss. Work has been supportive and understanding over the last twelve months. But I worry their patience with me is wearing thin. They never make me feel that way; I just can't imagine it's easy covering for me whenever Finn has a meltdown.

A corporate company wouldn't be as lenient, and I thank my lucky stars Finer Furnishings is a family-run store. I'd started working there years ago as my first after-school job, and I never left. When I graduated high school, they offered me a full-time managerial position, so I stayed.

"Hi, Maz, I'm sorry for the late notice, but Finn isn't doing so good today. I can't come in," I speak into the phone while picking at my nails, sure that today is the day they have enough of me.

"Okay, honey, you just take care of that boy of yours. We'll sort something out."

I sigh heavily, relief and guilt washing over me. "Thanks, Maz. I'm sorry."

"Don't. You're all that boy has. You know how we feel about Finn. Just look after him, and I'll look after things here," she says.

"Thank you," I murmur then end the call.

I take another minute to pull myself together before going down to Finn's room and knocking on his door. "Can I come in?" I ask.

"No," he yells back.

"Please, Finn, let me in, buddy. I just wanna sit with you," I tell him, pressing my forehead against the cool surface of the door.

A minute passes, then I hear the lock disengage, and I push on the handle to let myself in. Finn's back sitting in the corner of his bed that's tucked against two walls. He looks so small, so helpless.

I crawl across to him and pull him into my side. "What are we going to do, bud?"

He shrugs against me, mumbling, "I don't know."

Ruffling his hair, I sigh. "Me either, buddy, but we'll figure it out. I promise."

"I wish we didn't have to," he sniffles into my shoulder, and I squeeze him tighter.

Inside, I know there's nobody else who could take care of Finn the way I can. We don't have any other family left. Finn has no grandparents on his father's side, and I'd never bothered to find out what happened to them when I had the chance. My own parents both passed when I was fifteen, within a few months of each other. I'm a change-of-life baby. My mother was fifty-five when she had me, and my father was already in his early sixties.

We sit in silence for the next half hour, then Finn's little body relaxes against me, and his breathing evens out. I press a kiss to his crown. My beautiful boy.

I know why Jacq left him with me now. We need each other. As long as I've got Finn, I've still got my sister too. And so long as he has me, he'll have his mom.

Chapter Three

Victoria

Twelve Years Ago . . .

Finn and I are sitting at the table, eating Cocoa Puffs for breakfast, when I ask, "So, what do you want to do for your birthday this year?"

He looks at me briefly then back to his bowl. "I want to move," he whispers.

I can't have heard him right; this is Jacq's house, and he wants to move? I don't understand. "I'm sorry, I didn't hear you, buddy."

His big brown eyes meet mine, and he swallows hard. "I want to move," he repeats.

Trying not to let my shock show, I shovel another spoonful of cereal into my mouth. When I swallow, he's still looking at me, uncertainty filling his gaze. I put my spoon down and steeple my fingers over my bowl. "Why?" When his face falls, I hurry to continue, "I'm not saying no; I'm just asking why, that's all."

His shoulders relax, and he mimics my pose. "I want to go somewhere where nobody knows what happened to Mom. I want to be a normal boy, but people still feel sorry for me and treat me differently here."

I nod because I know what he means. It's been two years, and we still get sympathetic stares when we're at the grocery store or walking down the main street. Maybe a fresh start would be good for both of us. "Where would you like to go?" I ask.

Finn scratches his chin, shrugging. "Somewhere far away."

I frown. "I'm open to the idea of moving, Finn, but we don't have to go far away to start over, you know. Hell, we could even stay here, and you could just change schools if you want."

He shakes his head. "No, that won't work. The neighbors still know, and the whole town knows. I want to go somewhere new and pretend that you're my real mom."

"Oh, okay," I mumble, my heart in my throat.

Finn's a smart and charismatic kid. Before Jacq died, he was the kid that all the others wanted to be friends with. But after, people didn't know how to be around him, around us. All his little friends eventually fell away, unsure of how to act around him after he'd been through something none of them could ever understand.

"So, you've been thinking about this for a while, huh?" I ask, stirring my cereal around my bowl.

He nods. "Yep, this is what I want for my birthday. I don't want a party or a cake. I just want to move."

I'll do anything for Finn, and if moving will help him, then that's what we're going to do. "Alright, buddy, should I get out a map? Or have you already thought of where you want to go?"

A broad smile—the likes of which I haven't seen on him in a really long time—stretches across his face. "I've been Googling a few places."

I'll pack up and go wherever he wants if it means he'll smile like that again. I get up and fetch my laptop, bringing it back over to sit beside him. "Okay, show me what you got."

Finn beams at me, then his arms are around my neck, squeezing. "Thank you, Tory."

SIX WEEKS LATER...

"That's the last of it, Miss Dixon. Is there anything else you'd like us to change around for you before we head out?" the mover asks, carrying in the large box with the TV inside.

"No thanks, I think we're good," I tell him, turning in a full circle to take in our new home in Shiloh Springs.

"Okay then, we'll be off. Have fun unpacking," he says after placing the TV on the floor by an outlet in the living room. Then he's gone, and it's just me and Finn.

"You pick your bedroom yet?" I call to Finn as I make my way down the hall to find him.

"Yup." His voice guides me down to the last door at the end of the hallway.

Leaning against the frame, I cross my arms. "Why this one?"

He's looking out the window. "I like the tree," he says, gesturing with his chin to the large oak that sits between the fence and the house.

I smile. He used to climb trees all the time—before we lost Jacq. "Maybe you can show me how to climb it," I joke.

He laughs softly. "Nah, you're too old. You'll break a hip if you fall."

I gasp. "I am not old! You're going to pay for that, you little punk," I say right before I pounce, grabbing him by the waist and pulling him to the floor to engage in a good old-fashioned round of tickle torture.

"I'm sorry! I'm sorry! You're not old! I take it back!" he yells as my fingers go to work on his rib cage.

I pause. "You mean it?" I ask with a raised brow.

Finn's smile is downright devious as he chuckles, "Nope."

"That's it! You're going to get it now!" I threaten.

But just as I'm about to attack, a knock sounds through the house from the front door. Relief fills Finn's eyes. "Ha!" he shouts then scrambles to his feet and runs out of the room.

By the time I make it to the front door, he's already swung it open.

There's a woman standing on the other side, holding a plate of cookies. "Hi, I'm Vera," she says, then she steps to the side, revealing a boy about Finn's age. "And this is Weston. We live next door. Thought we'd come by and welcome you to the neighborhood."

"Oh, hi. I'm Tory, and this is Finn," I say, placing my hand on Finn's shoulder. "We haven't unpacked yet, so I can't offer you anything, but you're welcome to come inside."

Vera smiles and shakes her head. "Oh no, that's okay, love. How about you and Finn come for dinner tonight? That will be one less thing you need to worry about today," she offers with a wink. "It's been a while since we've moved, but I still remember what a hellish task it was."

I laugh; she's totally right. This moving thing sucks ass. "Amen to that! And thank you; that would be amazing."

Vera nods then grins. "Okay, well, come around any time after five. We live in the house to your right," she says, gesturing in that direction.

"Thanks," I call out after her as she leaves.

The boy, Weston, remains standing on the stoop, a shy smile playing at the corner of his mouth. I look to Finn who's eyeing the boy curiously.

I nudge his side. "Why don't you see if Weston wants to hang out while you start unpacking your room?"

Weston's eyes light up. "I don't mind helping," he says to Finn.

A small smile lifts the side of Finn's mouth as he slides his hands into his pockets. "Okay. This way." He gestures with his chin for Weston to follow him, and he does.

A couple of hours later, I've finally finished unpacking the kitchen. *I should have paid the movers extra and gotten them to unpack for me.*

I'm just reaching up to put the last glass on the shelf by the fridge when the boys come in, chatting animatedly between themselves.

Pure, sweet relief fills me. Finn's made a friend, and it's only our first day here.

"Can we have a drink, Tor—uh, Mom?" Finn asks. He's giving me the *eye*—the one that says *just go with it...*

I scrunch my brows then remember he wants people to think I'm his real mom. I swallow past the lump of emotion clogging my throat. "We've only got tap water, bud. We'll have to go grocery shopping tomorrow."

"Oh, yeah, I forgot." Turning to Weston, he says, "Sorry, looks like it's water or nothin'."

Weston shrugs. "That's okay. Water's good."

Finn smiles widely. "We'll take two waters please."

I can't resist ruffling his messy hair. "Comin' right up." I go about getting them their drinks, glancing at my watch as I hand them over. "When you finish your drink, you should go take a quick shower, Finn. We're going to go over to Weston's house for dinner soon."

Weston smiles at Finn. "I have all the Avenger figurines. You want to play when we get to my place?"

Finn's eyes widen. "Awesome! I want Thor, though; he's the coolest."

I clear my throat. "Forgetting your manners there, Finn. They're Weston's toys. You don't tell him which one you're going to play with; you ask."

His cheeks pink up with embarrassment. "Sorry," he mumbles to Weston who shakes his head.

"Nah, it's okay. I like Captain America the best, anyway."

"Alright, shower now, Finn," I instruct then turn to Weston. "Can you head home and let your mom know we'll be over in half an hour?"

He nods with vigor. "Okay, see you soon, Finn." Then, he runs out the back sliding door.

I walk over to check out how he gets back into his own yard and catch him slipping through a gate joining the two yards that I hadn't noticed before. *That'll be convenient for the boys.*

Finn gets out of the shower a few minutes later, calling, "Tory, where are my clothes?"

"Give me a sec, bud; I'm looking now," I yell back, then my eyes land on a box marked in Finn's handwriting: *Finn's Threadz.*

Laughing, I pick it up and take it to his room. "Found your *threadz*," I tease.

He smiles. "Sounds cooler than clothes," he says with a shrug as I drop the box at the end of his bed.

"I'll make your bed when we get home, okay?" I tell him over my shoulder as I leave his room to go in search of my own clothes.

Twenty minutes later, we're standing on Vera's porch in fresh clothes, a bottle of wine I found while unpacking the kitchen stuff that afternoon clutched in my hand.

Can't go wrong with wine, right?

Chapter Four

Victoria

Ten Years Ago . . .

"She's so pretty!" Weston says as the boys sit at the kitchen counter and wait for their afternoon snack.

"Who's so pretty?" I ask while getting out the bread and fixings for their sandwiches.

Vera works until five-thirty most days, so Weston comes to our place after school each afternoon instead of going to the after-school care program. I make the boys a snack to hold them over until dinner time, then they do their homework together before hitting the XBOX.

Finn blushes furiously. "No one," he mutters.

My eyes light up. *Does he have a crush?* He hasn't told me about any girls lately. "Do you have a new girlfriend?" I tease.

He groans, "Mom!"

Weston throws his head back, laughing. "Carrie Tate asked Finn out today."

"Oh, did she now?" I say, putting the finishing touches on their sandwiches. "And what did you say?" I ask Finn. When he doesn't answer, I hold his plate hostage. "Tell me or I eat this delicious sandwich."

"I said no," he grumbles.

I hand over his plate and watch him dig in as soon as it hits the counter in front of him. "Why'd you say no?" Finn shoots Weston a look—one I recognize. "Spill," I demand, narrowing my eyes.

Finn shakes his head at Weston then glares for good measure.

Weston ignores him, grinning at me. "He likes Kelly Kimmons."

I gasp, genuinely shocked. "I thought you said Kelly was fourteen?"

Both the boys shrug. "So?" Weston voices what I'm pretty sure they're both thinking.

I scrunch my nose. "But you guys are only twelve. Isn't that gross? She's older than you."

They both crack up laughing, bits of lettuce spraying from their still full mouths.

"That just means she has bigger boobs," Finn says when he's finished laughing, obviously getting over his bout of embarrassment on the subject.

My hands shoot up to plug my ears. "Ewww!" I cry, and they continue to laugh as they get up from the counter and take their school bags to the table to start their homework.

A sense of dread washes over me. *Isn't twelve too young to be noticing things like boobs?*

I knew they'd start paying attention to girls soon, but twelve? I thought I had at least two more years before I had to worry about this stuff. I tidy the kitchen while stewing over this new development. Does this mean we need to have *The Talk?* God, I hope not. I am not ready for that.

When Vera gets home from work that night, I decide a little parental advice is in order.

I wait until the boys retreat to the living room to play the newest game I'd gotten for Finn's XBOX, then I broach the topic with Vera. "Have you had *The Talk* with Weston yet?"

Vera stops washing the plate in her hands and looks up at me. "*The Talk?*" she asks with a raised brow.

I nod. "Yeah, *The Talk.*"

She slowly rinses the suds from the plate then puts it with the others in the drying rack. After wiping her hands, she goes to the cupboard that stores the wine glasses and pulls two down, then she fills them both to the brim. I watch her silently, waiting for her to explain what she's doing.

When she's done, she turns to me and hands me a glass. "I think a conversation of this magnitude will require this," she says, gesturing to our nearly overflowing wine glasses, "and it's probably best to have it out of earshot of nosey boys."

I wave that last part off. "They're so absorbed in that new game we could be talking about childbirth and periods and they wouldn't notice."

We glance in the boys' direction to check my theory, and sure enough, they haven't so much as flinched. They are too focused on the TV screen in front of them.

Vera frowns. "Fair enough, but let's go outside anyway. I'm paranoid." She laughs softly, and I follow her out the back sliding door to our small patio.

Closing the door behind me, I let out a sigh. "They were talking about boobs today," I whine. "Boobs! They're only twelve. Do I need to have *The Talk* with him already?

Because I don't think I'm ready for that, V, I really don't," I say as I plonk down in one of the timber outdoor chairs I'd purchased when we bought the house.

Vera sighs, too, then takes a hefty swig of her wine. "I was afraid this day was coming sooner rather than later. I was hoping Wes' father would take the lead on this one, but you and I both know that sorry son of a bitch would probably tell the boy to go out and sow his wild oats as much and as often as possible. And I'd end up a grandmother before I'm forty."

We both laugh, but the reality of the situation is a very real possibility for Vera. Her ex is a Grade-A asshole who skipped out on her when Weston was just a little baby.

I take a gulp of my wine. "What am I supposed to say to him?"

Vera shrugs. "I don't think it's worth worrying about just yet. I mean, boys will be boys, and at this stage, they're just noticing these things. I think we're still safe for now. Just start thinking about what your parents said to you."

I cringe. "I was a surprise baby. Mom was mid-fifties when she had me, so I was definitely unexpected. Jacq had the sex talk with me when I was about thirteen, I think. And it went something like, 'Don't ever be alone with a boy, or he will try to put his penis in your vagina. Then you will get fat and have to push a whole baby out of your teeny tiny vagina.'"

Vera bursts out laughing, wine spraying out of her mouth all over the patio. "Wow, that was graphic," she manages to gasp out after she finishes choking.

"No kidding. Needless to say, I was terrified of being alone with boys until I realized that not every boy in the world wanted to inseminate me," I say with a smile. I still remember being horrified at the prospect of pushing a whole baby out of my tiny vagina. The thought still makes me feel queasy.

Vera continues laughing. "You gotta admit, it was a good method to avoid teen pregnancy."

I nod. "Yeah, it was," I say with a chuckle, remembering how I'd freaked out on the first boy who tried to kiss me when I was fourteen. I'd threatened to kick him in the nuts if he even thought about pulling his penis out.

"Maybe, when the time comes, you should open with a similar line. Something like, 'Don't ever be alone with a girl, or she will try to get in your pants so she can have your baby, and you'll have to watch the baby come out of what you once thought was a special place. And it will ruin all vaginas for you forever.'" Vera laughs to herself.

A loud snort is my only response—and hysterical laughter.

Chapter Five

Victoria

Seven Years Ago . . .

"Mom, have you seen my sunglasses?" Finn calls out from his room.

"Where you last put them," I call back from the kitchen where I'm finishing up dinner prep for that night.

Finn comes stalking down the hallway. "I can't find them," he huffs with his hands on his hips. "I've looked everywhere!" he says, gesturing to the entire house with his hand.

Smirking at him, I can't help but be a smartass. "What about the mirror?"

He frowns. "What?"

"Did you look for them in the mirror?" I hedge.

His eyes narrow then light with realization and embarrassment. He gingerly lifts his hand to feel the top of his head, and sure enough, he finds his sunglasses.

"Thanks," he grumbles as he turns away, about to head back down the hallway.

"Bit nervous for your first date, huh?" I call after him. It is adorable how jittery he has been all day.

He stops in his tracks and slowly turns to me, his eyes on the ground. "Do I look okay?" he asks quietly.

I walk toward him, and when I reach him, I lift his chin so he is looking at me, even though I don't really need to; he outgrew me six months ago. "Finn, you're a stud, buddy." I check out his outfit. "And a fashionable one, at that. Anyone would think you have connections in the clothing industry." I grin.

A blush fills his cheeks. "Thanks. It is kinda handy having you manage Taylors."

I shrug. "I had to get the job there. I need the employee discount to afford all the clothes I've had to buy you since you started growing so damn fast. Have we measured you recently?"

Finn's chest puffs out with pride. "Wes measured me in gym yesterday. I've hit six feet."

My eyes bug out of my head. "Steroids make your package shrink, you know. Lay off the juice, dude."

Finn rolls his eyes at me, but before he can hit me with his own smartass comment, Weston enters through the back sliding door. I look over my shoulder to him. "Is my boy a stud or what?" I say, gesturing to Finn with my chin.

Weston gags. "I'm not in the habit of checking out my best friend—or any dudes, just for the record. But if I did"—he looks Finn up and down—"I suppose he'd do."

Finn flips Weston the bird. "I'm a catch, and you know it."

I laugh and leave them to their bickering. I won't admit it to Finn, but I am nervous as hell about his first date. He is taking a girl in his grade to the movies. When he'd asked me if I would drop them off then pick them up afterwards, I'd happily agreed, only because I want to check her out for myself and make sure she is good enough for my boy. And to make sure she isn't a little skank that would try to rub him up during the movie.

In the car on the way to pick her up, I decide now is the right time to have *The Talk*. "So, with this being your first date and all, I'm obligated to make sure you're aware of sex and all that it entails."

Finn chokes on his chewing gum. "MOM!" he yells, looking at me like I've grown a second head.

"What?" I ask. "Don't tell me you didn't see this conversation coming, Finn," I shoot back.

His face is bright red—his ears too—and he starts to pick at his fingernails. "I'm not going to have sex with her; we're going to the movies, not a hotel."

I snort. "You don't have to go to a hotel to have sex. Besides, that's not what I'm saying. I'm just making sure you know the *ins* and *outs* of it, and I want you to know you can talk to me about this stuff. You can ask me anything you want, anytime. Okay? That's all I'm saying."

He nods and looks out the window. "Yeah, I know. And I will—when I'm ready. But I'm not yet. I haven't even kissed a girl. One step at a time, okay?"

Relief floods my system. He isn't thinking about having sex yet. I send a silent prayer up, thanking God. "Okay," I say back softly and leave the topic there.

To my utter surprise, the girl he is going out with is a

geek. Like, a glasses-wearing, braces-on-teeth, double-braids, and mismatching-socks kind of geek. I'd honestly be shocked if she doesn't have at least one book in that bag she's carrying.

I like her instantly.

I wait in the car while Finn goes up and knocks on the front door of her house and speaks to her father. I can tell he's nervous. He keeps his eyes down and nods a lot. Then, the girl comes to the door, kisses her father on the cheek, and takes Finn's outstretched hand, leaving her father standing in the open doorway with a scowl on his face.

I feel for the guy; I really do. But seeing the smile on Finn's face makes everything going on inside of me settle.

Finn opts to sit in the backseat with his date, making me feel like a chauffeur.

"Mom, this is Nixie. Nixie, this is my mom, Tory," Finn introduces us as I drive.

I glance at them in the rearview mirror. "Nice to meet you, Nixie." She's blushing furiously, but the smile on her face matches Finn's.

"Nice to meet you too, Tory," she whispers back.

They speak quietly between themselves for the remainder of the ten-minute drive to the cinema. When I pull up out front, I hand Finn a fifty. "Get all the good stuff. Lots of chocolate; chicks love chocolate." I wink, and Finn laughs.

"Thanks, Mom. The movie finishes in two hours, so we'll just meet you out here, yeah?"

I nod. "Have fun. Don't do anything I wouldn't do," I call as he closes the door on my words.

As soon as they are on the sidewalk, a tear slides down my cheek. He is growing up so fast. I wish Jacq was here to see what an amazing young man he has become. She would be so proud of him.

Over the next few weeks, I see a lot of Nixie. She starts walking home from school with the boys and doing her homework with them in the afternoons. Then, she has a cup of tea with me and talks about whatever new book she's obsessing over.

I really like her; she is a lovely girl. I'm still surprised that, out of all the girls I know were after Finn, he chose Nixie. She is pretty, but not in the typical way. It makes my heart so full that Finn could see past the superficial to how truly beautiful Nix is. She is outgoing, but not overly confident. And best of all, she looks at Finn like the sun rises and sets with him.

They've been dating for about three months when I learn that the other girls at school have been hassling Nixie because of her relationship with Finn. She isn't popular and doesn't fit in with any of the cliques. Their relationship defies the age-old high school rules about popular kids only dating other popular kids.

Finn is popular. He and Weston practically rule their grade. I don't know how, but they do. They're both key players on the football team, so I suspect that and their good looks are the reason behind their popularity.

And I'm not just being biased; Finn is a really good-looking kid—Weston too. And the girls at their school notice. Weston loves the attention, but Finn isn't such a fan.

One afternoon when Finn comes home, I can feel the change in him before he utters a single word. "What happened?" I ask when he comes inside and flops down on the couch without greeting me like he usually does.

He stretches out along the couch and throws his arm

over his eyes. "Nixie won't be coming around anymore. I'm sorry. I know you liked her."

I frown. "What's going on, Finn?" A shuddering sigh escapes him, and I sit on the edge of the couch and lift his arm off his face to find tears gathered in the corners of his eyes. I haven't seen him cry in years.

His Adam's apple bobs. "She broke up with me." A single tear slides down his cheek.

My heart breaks for him. I'm every bit as upset up by this as he is. "Oh, honey," I say as I lay my head down on his chest and wrap my arms around him. "I'm so, so sorry."

Finn wraps his arms around my back. "Me too," he murmurs quietly.

He's silent for a long time, then says, "I didn't even know she was getting so much shit for being with me. Why are girls such fucking bitches?" He sucks in a trembling breath. "She couldn't handle it anymore, being tormented every day. And it's all my fault."

"It is not your fault Finn," I promise him. "Teenage girls can be vicious, I don't know why, maybe it's hormones or something. But I do know how much Nixie cares about you, she wouldn't have broken up with you if it wasn't really bad."

He nods. "Yeah, I know. That's why I'm letting her go without a fight."

I feel his chest heave as he attempts to control his emotions, and I break inside a little more.

Weston comes over later that afternoon and tries to cheer Finn up, but he won't have it. And I don't blame him. He needs time to deal. He tries to send Weston home, but he refuses to go. "No, man, I'll just hang out."

I hear their exchange when I go to take snacks in to them. I pause at the partially open door and listen.

"You have a date with Chelsea tonight; you've been stringing her along for ages. Just go and put the poor girl out of her misery," Finn says.

Weston scoffs. "She's wanted a piece of me for months; she can wait another night before I give it to her. You're my brother. What could be more important than you right now? Not a piece of ass I can tap whenever I want."

My eyes grow wide. What he just said was incredibly sweet, then he followed it with a wad of information I really didn't want to know. I push the door open the rest of the way while clearing my throat to announce my entrance.

Both their heads swivel in my direction, and Weston grins at me. "Hey, Tory," he says with a smirk.

I narrow my eyes on the little bastard. He knows I heard their conversation. I'm both embarrassed for having been caught eavesdropping and grossed out at the thought of fifteen-year-old Weston having sex.

Raising my brow, I give him a pointed look. "You little slutski," I accuse.

And he grins wider. "Don't worry, Tor. No high school girl will ever measure up to you."

My face scrunches up. "Eww. That's just...yuck. Don't say that kind of shit to me. It's weird and gross."

Finn's fist shoots out and punches Weston in the shoulder as he laughs half-heartedly. "Dude! That's my mom, asshole."

Weston rubs his shoulder and chuckles. "It's not my fault you've got a hot mom, dude."

I plonk the tray of snacks on Finn's desk and leave the room as Finn flies toward Weston with his fists already clenched and ready to give his best friend a beat down. "I'm out," I say as I leave the room, smiling as I walk down the hallway. Weston has certainly taken Finn's mind off Nixie, if only for a few minutes.

Chapter Six

Victoria

Six Years Ago . . .

Grabbing my keys out of the bowl on the side table, I go to open the front door. I'm actually running on time for a change. But when I swing it open, Weston is standing on the other side. "Finn's not home, he got called in for an extra shift today," I tell him as I squeeze past him and close the door behind me.

His big shoulders drop. "Shit," he mutters under his breath and releases a defeated sigh.

I turn around to look up at him; he and Finn are both well over six feet tall, and I'm only just over five myself. It irritates me immensely. Trying to maintain an authoritative presence with two sixteen-year-olds that tower over you is not easy.

But when I really look into his face, I notice something isn't right. I glance at my watch. If I don't leave right now, I'll be late. I sigh. "Come on," I say and take him by the bicep, guiding him to my car. "If I don't go now, I'll miss my appointment, and I've been waiting for this for ages. So you can talk while I drive, okay?"

He nods and gets in the front passenger seat while I round the hood and climb in behind the wheel of my Love Bug. The boys usually make fun of me for my little car, but Weston doesn't have any smartass comments about having to fold himself in half to fit inside today.

I glance at him, worried, as I pull out of the driveway. "What's up, big man? No jokes about my beast of a car today?"

He's staring at his hands folded in his lap. It's freaking me out. Weston is never this quiet. I reach over to touch his arm when he blurts out, "Jessie thinks she's pregnant."

My foot slips off the accelerator, and the car jerks violently before I regain my bearings and shift the gear down to match the slowed speed before she stalls out. "I'm sorry, what did you just say?"

His lifts his troubled eyes to meet my wide ones. "Jessie, a girl I was kinda dating last month... she thinks she's pregnant."

I focus on the road in front of me as best I can while processing the information. Why is he talking to me about this and not Vera? This is definitely a mother-son conversation. "Have you told your mom?" I ask softly.

He shakes his head. "Not yet; she's working late." He shrugs then drops his shoulders again. "What am I going to do, Tory?" he says with a hitch in his voice.

Taking a few calming breaths, I glance at him from the corner of my eye again. His hands are in fists in his lap, and his jaw is clenched tight. Every muscle in his body is held rigid. I reach for him again and touch his hand. "It's going to be okay. No matter what happens, we'll figure it out."

His eyes meet mine for a brief moment, then he nods once before turning to look out the window.

When I try to move my hand away from his, he wraps his fingers through mine and holds it tight. "Weston, I mean it; we'll figure it out. You're not the first person to have the rug pulled out from under their feet. You'll find your footing again. Trust me. I mean, look at me, look at your mom. Neither of us expected to be single mothers, yet here we are, making the best of what life gave us," I say and squeeze his hand.

His Adam's apple bobs as he swallows hard. "Okay," he whispers then clears his throat. "Where are we going, anyway?" he says, looking back at me.

I smile brightly. "I'm getting a tattoo!" I tell him, letting my excitement show.

His eyes widen. "What? You're a mom. Moms don't get tattoos."

Rolling my eyes, I pull into a parking spot in front of The Parlor, then turn to face him as I turn off the ignition. "Do I look like a normal mom to you?" I ask.

He frowns and shakes his head. "Uh, no. Definitely not." Then, his lips lift in a sly smirk.

I raise a brow. "I'm going to take that as a compliment, whether you meant it as one or not. My point is, I've wanted this for a long time, and I rarely do anything for myself. So I'm doing it. Right now. With or without you," I say as I open my door then step out of Love Bug and slam the door behind me.

Weston gets out a moment later, wearing a ridiculously huge grin. "What are you smiling about?" I snap. I hate that his words got to me; I am a damn good mom. So, I'm not a normal mom, but Finn's and my situation isn't like everyone else's.

"Nothin'," he replies, not losing the damn smile.

"Whatever," I mutter and hit the lock button on my keys then start for the entrance to the shop with Weston on my heel.

WESTON SITS IN THE SEATING AREA WHILE A CHICK CALLED Talia gets to work on a beautiful dreamcatcher tattoo on my forearm. It will completely cover the scar that brings up the painful memory of the day we lost Jacq every time I see it. The nightmares still haunt my dreams every so often.

It was after a particularly vivid nightmare that I decided to get the dreamcatcher. Jacq had a small one hanging off the rearview mirror in her car, and it stood out to me in that dream for some reason.

When it's done, I call Weston over to have a look before Talia wraps it. "Like it?" I ask.

His fingertip traces the design gently, then he looks into my eyes. "Your scar?"

I nod. "Yeah." The compassion shining in his gaze is too much, and I have to look away. Weston can see inside of me, and it scares the crap out of me. He's too young for us to share that kind of connection.

When I'm finished, we head back out to my car, and slide inside without a word. Glancing at Weston as I pull out of my parking spot, I notice the smile he was wearing earlier is long gone.

We drive home in silence.

Pulling up in the driveway, I grab his arm as he goes to slip out of the car before I even turn her off. "Wait," I say, and he pauses but doesn't turn back to face me. I sigh, leaning back against my headrest. I don't know if he's upset about my snapping at him earlier or the potentially pregnant chick.

"You can talk to me; you know that, right?" I say only just loud enough for him to hear me.

Leaving his door open, one foot on the concrete drive still, he relaxes back into his seat. "Yeah, Tory, I know. Honestly, I would rather talk to you about it than Mom. You're more of a friend. Like, you would give good advice without ripping my dick off the way Mom probably will. And you know I wouldn't have said anything about Jessie if I didn't think I could talk to you."

Right, of course. "So you wanna talk now?" I ask.

He runs his hand through his styled hair. "I don't know. I mean, there isn't anything I can do. So what good is talking about it going to do?"

"It will get it off your chest," I suggest. "So, when did she tell you?"

"This afternoon, after school. She texted me, telling me she needed to talk and it was really important, so I met her, and she just dropped it on me," he says.

"Okay, well, this might be a stupid question, but are you sure she's pregnant, and are you sure it's yours if she is?" I've gotten over my initial shock and am in fix-it mode now.

Weston scratches the side of his neck. "Well, we had sex, so yeah, it could be mine. But I swear I tarp up every single time, though."

"You know condoms aren't 100% effective, right?" I deadpan.

His face pales. "What?"

I lick my lips and sit up straighter in my seat. "There is always a small chance that they could break, that kind of thing."

He nods, visibly relaxing. "Oh, well yeah, but that's never happened to me."

I chew my bottom lip, thinking it over. "So how do you know it's yours then? Or that she's even really pregnant? Did you break up with her, or did she break up with you?"

A grimace covers his face. "We weren't exactly dating, so we didn't exactly break up."

I cover my face with my hands. "Such a slutski," I murmur under my breath.

Weston obviously hears me, though, because he responds, "Why am *I* the slut? They want it, and I give it to them. It's a mutual thing. We both get off, then I get gone."

A shudder runs down my spine. "Gross."

"What? What's gross about that? Everyone needs to get off sometimes, Tory—even you. I don't see what's gross about it," he says genuinely.

"What's gross is that you're sixteen, Weston, and you've slept with how many girls? That's what's gross. And you think sex is just about getting off. It's not, FYI. And the fact that you think it is just proves you shouldn't be out having it. Oh, and don't ever talk about me and then you getting off in the same sentence again. That is super gross." I shudder again.

He rolls his eyes at me now. "When you're sixteen, sex *is* just about getting off. I don't expect to fall in love with any of these girls, and I've only slept with four. Each time, we both knew the score."

I wave him off. "Whatever, I don't want to know more

about your sex life than necessary. My point is, did you stop sleeping with her, or did she stop sleeping with you?"

He scratches the back of his neck. "I stopped. She was getting too clingy, texting me all the damn time, wanting to know what I was doing and if she could come hang out with me and Finn. That's not how I roll, and she knew it. So I cut her off."

"The way you talk about her deeply disturbs me, just so you know." And it really did. He cut her off? What the hell kind of way to speak about the girl he'd been sleeping with is that? "We'll talk about your utter disrespect of women at another time, but for right now, I'm going to give you my honest opinion of the situation."

Weston nods eagerly, awaiting my take on all that he has imparted to me. "Okay, hit me."

"Go buy a pregnancy test, take it to her, and tell her to take it with you there, like, outside the door or something. I think you've hurt her and she wants payback, or she is upset that you broke it off with her and she wants you back so she's trying to do that the only way she can think of."

He frowns. "Seriously? You think she's just fucking with me? That's pretty messed up."

I raise a brow. "So is fucking her then not returning her calls."

"Touché," he says then climbs out of Love Bug, but he pokes his head back in before he goes back home. "Thanks, Tory."

I wink. "You're welcome; let me know how it goes."

When I open the front door and come face to face with Finn's bare ass, I scream, "What the hell, Finn?!" I turn my back on him and face the closed door. "What are you doing? Put some damn pants on."

"Uh, can you give us a minute?" Finn's voice sounds small and embarrassed.

"Yep, you betcha. Call out when you're decent. We are going to be having a serious conversation as soon as clothes are back in play." Then I re-open the front door, step back out onto the porch and slam it behind me again.

A minute or two later, I hear Finn call out, "Decent," and I turn the handle and let myself back in.

My jaw drops when I spot Nixie sitting on the couch beside Finn. Her face is as beet red as his. "Wha—uh—I'm so confused," I stutter. "I wish I hadn't seen what I clearly just saw, but I'm happy to see you, Nix."

Her shoulders relax in relief, and she gives me a small finger wave. "It's good to see you too, Tory. Sorry about"—her hand gestures between the two of them—"this," she finishes with a grimace.

"Me too," I mutter.

Finn is smiling brightly, and I glare at him as I plonk down on the couch that I had not just seen him having sex on. "You're paying to have that couch cleaned," I tell him. "I watch Netflix on that couch!" I whine. "Couldn't you have taken it to your bedroom? I mean, seriously, what made you think the couch was a good place for you two to be bumping uglies?"

Nixie's eyes bounce between Finn and me with a puzzled expression on her pretty face.

I stand up. "You know what, don't answer that; I can't deal with this today. I'm exhausted. I just got an awesome tattoo, by the way. Just so you know. I was going to surprise you with it, but you don't get to see the awesomeness until later now."

"You what?" Finn asks.

I hold my hand up in his face. "Talk to the hand 'cause the face ain't listening. Now if you'll excuse me, I'm going to go scrub my eyeballs with bleach, if you don't mind," I tell him as I walk down the hallway. Every time I close my damn eyes, I can see Finn thrusting into Nixie, and I want to hurl.

My day can't possibly get any worse. Talking sex and babies with Weston, then seeing Finn's ass as he pumped into his ex-girlfriend on my Netflix couch. I need a huge glass of wine and a scalding hot bath to wash it all away.

The next morning, Weston comes over to tell me that he'd gone to see Jessie last night, and she'd broken down crying and confessed to making it up to try to get him back.

"Told ya," I say when he finishes giving me the low down. "I'm hoping this has served as some kind of lesson to you about the way you treat girls."

He nods. "For sure. I'll keep it between me and my hand for a while now."

I gag. "You have a problem with boundaries, Weston."

He laughs. "Nah, I just like seeing the look on your face when I talk about sex or my dick."

I throw my hands up. "Okay, this conversation is well and truly over. Get out of my house now, you little perv." I shoo him away, and he goes, laughing his ass off the whole way.

"Was that Wes?" Finn's voice comes from behind me, making me jump out of my skin.

My hand flies to my heart. "Jesus, Finn! You scared the crap out of me." I haven't seen him since I left him in the living room last night.

He laughs. "Sorry. Why are you so on edge anyway?"

I scoff. "Oh, I don't know, I walked in on you having sex with your ex-girlfriend last night, and I had to talk about sex and babies with Weston because you were too busy off having sex!" I exclaim. Then I add, "What's with that, by the way? Since when are you and Nixie back together? And when did you start having sex?!"

Finn blushes and rubs the back of his neck. "We've kinda been back together for a while now. We've just kept it quiet."

I frown, hurt he felt he couldn't confide in me. "Why wouldn't you tell me?"

He sighs heavily. "We didn't tell anybody. Not even Wes knows. I can't let those bitches get to her again. They made her life hell before and all behind my back. I had no idea. I can't take that risk. It took months just to get her to talk to me again." His tone has changed as he speaks, revealing how strongly he feels for her.

Sighing, I walk to him and wrap my arms around his waist. "Okay, I understand. But keep it in your pants when you're sitting on my couch next time."

He laughs and wraps his arms around me. "Deal."

"You're still paying to have it cleaned. I'm not sitting on it until I'm sure it's free of all bodily fluids," I tell him in all seriousness.

Again, Finn laughs. "Do you know how weird we are? We're hugging while you're telling me to make sure the couch is jizz free."

Now, I laugh. Taking a small step back but keeping my arms around him, I tell him honestly, "You and me, we'll never be like everyone else. We'll always be a bit weird. You will always be my son, but you were my little buddy first. I love you, and I want you to be happy. Me going crazy because you're sexually active isn't going to help either of us. I just wish you'd told me."

He smiles. "That would have been a really awkward conversation," he chuckles.

I scoff. "No worse than what I walked in on last night. I never want to see your bare ass again, especially not while you're having sex on my couch," I shoot back with an exaggerated shudder.

Finn smirks. "Sorry about that."

I roll my eyes. "Sure you are."

"I like our weird," he says, then he pulls me back into his arms and gives me a quick squeeze before releasing me and heading into the kitchen to ransack the cupboards for breakfast.

Chapter Seven

Victoria

Five Years Ago . . .

Makeup is not my friend. I hate the stuff. But when you haven't slept well for the last week because of a killer sinus infection, and you have huge black bags under your eyes, it's a necessary evil, lest I terrify my fellow employees.

Standing in the bathroom in front of the mirror after having applied a liberal amount of concealer under my eyes, I pick up the next product on the vanity to help hide my panda eyes.

"What the hell did you do to your face?"

I spin around and come face to face with Weston. "What are you doing here?" I snap, embarrassed at being seen like *this*.

He eyes me. "You look like shit, Tory. Why are you out of bed?"

I raise a brow. "I have to go to work. And you didn't

answer me. What are you doing here? It's not even seven AM."

"I know what time it is. Finn and I have an early practice this morning before school. But seriously, you look like shit; you should call in sick," he says, the look in his eyes conveying his concern for me.

I heave a sigh. "Believe me, if I could crawl back in bed right now, I would. But I've already had a week off, and we're short-staffed." I turn my back on him and continue applying the array of makeup spread across the top of the vanity.

Looking back into the mirror, I can see Weston still standing in the open doorway behind me, arms crossed over his broad chest. "Don't worry, I'll hide in my office most of the day," I say with a small smile I don't feel.

He gives a slight nod to my reflection then turns and stalks away. A minute later, he returns with a glass of water and some pills. "Here, take these. If you take them now, it will give them time to kick in before you have to leave. You shouldn't be driving when you're this sick."

I take the water, painkillers, and antibiotics he hands me gratefully. "Thanks," I murmur then down the lot in one go.

"I'll drop you at work on our way to practice. What time is your shift over?" he asks.

He's trying to take care of me, and I appreciate the gesture, but I don't need it, especially from a seventeen-year-old kid. I'm a grown woman, for goodness' sake. It's my job to take care of them, not the other way around. "It's fine, Weston; I can drive myself. Thanks for the pills."

He shakes his head and leaves the bathroom again, only to return this time with a sleepy Finn. Weston points at me. "Tell her she can't drive," he demands of Finn.

Finn rubs his eyes then focuses on me and balks. "What is on your face?"

I roll my eyes. "It's called makeup."

He scrunches up his nose. "Since when do you wear that crap?"

I'm beginning to get pissed. I spin around, and with my hands on my hips, I glare at the boys eyeing me like I've grown a second head. "I'm trying to look respectable for work, okay? I can't show up looking like I got in a fight with a freaking kangaroo and got punched in the face."

"You look like shit, Mom. Maybe you should stay home again?" Finn says.

My head is hurting too much to have this conversation again. "I've already explained to Mr. Nosey." I flick my hand toward Weston. "I have to go in today. We're short-staffed. I'll be in my office most of the day."

Weston leans over closer to Finn and turns his face away so I can't read his lips as he whispers in Finn's ear. Finn nods then eyes me again. "We'll drop you off. You shouldn't drive. Hell, you shouldn't be out of bed, let alone behind the wheel."

I stomp my foot like a petulant child. I am not happy about the reversal of roles going on right now. "Who's the parent here? Me, not you. I take care of you. You don't need to take care of me, Finn. And neither do you, Weston." My gaze flicks between the two of them.

Another thing I'm not too happy about is the whole giant thing these two have going on. I feel like a midget. It is hard to scold them when I have to literally look up to them.

Finn shakes his head at me then ruffles my hair. "We'll drive you," he says again, then they both walk out, leaving me fuming.

By the time I finish making my face look a little more respectable and emerge from the bathroom, all the fight has left me. I'm too tired to argue with them, so I accept the lift to work and tell Finn he can just pick me up after their practice in the afternoon.

That afternoon, however, Weston comes to pick me up, without Finn. I frown as I climb into his truck. "Where's Finn?"

"Sucking face with Nix. Where else?" he replies with a roll of his eyes.

I nod. "Sounds about right." I sigh and lay my head back against the headrest, closing my eyes. I am beyond exhausted.

I wake with a start a few minutes later. I feel Weston's hand wrap around my upper arm, giving me a little nudge. "We're home," he says quietly.

Shaking my head to push away the sleep from my mind, I clear my throat. "Thanks for the ride," I mutter as I climb out of the car and make my way over to my own house.

Weston comes up behind me, wrapping his arm around my shoulders as we walk. "You should have stayed home today. You look even worse than you did this morning, Tory."

I lean into his side. "Such a charmer you are; how do the girls resist you?" I mock with a yawn.

"I only turn it on for you, Tor; you're my girl," he says with a wicked gleam in his eyes, then he winks at me.

I chuckle softly. "And smooth too."

He shrugs his shoulder. "You know it. I'm a natural with the ladies. I've been practicing on you since I was ten." He smirks.

I roll my tired eyes. "Don't I know it."

Pulling the keys from my bag, Weston takes them from

me and opens the door. He leads me inside, straight to the couch. "You sit. I'll make you a cup of tea."

"Umm, okay..." I mumble, but I'm not going to complain. I am wiped, and a hot cuppa sounds great. I flop back against the soft cushions and close my eyes.

I like being looked after for a change. It feels good.

The boys have a big game coming up, and their coach has them pulling double practices this whole week, apparently. So that means that lucky me gets a ride to work with my seventeen-year-old son every morning until he deems me well enough to drive myself.

It is times like these that I hate Vera's work hours. If they were normal, I could just hitch a ride with her.

Chapter Eight

Victoria

Four Years Ago . . .

"So, what are we doing for your eighteenth?" I ask Finn over dinner about a month before the big day.

He shovels another forkful of steak into his mouth and contemplates my question as he chews. After swallowing, he says, "I was thinkin' I'd just hang out with Nixie."

Well, that hurts. "You don't want a party?" I've always thrown him kickass birthday parties.

"Don't look so sad," he laughs. "I just want to chill with Nix, that's all. You know how she is around crowds. She'll be uncomfortable, and I'll feel like a dick for putting her through it."

Finn and Nixie have kept their relationship a secret for a year since they got back together. She is too afraid to come out in the open with him after what she endured when they had first gotten together. And even after all this time, she still feels like he's out of her league.

He has bent over backwards, trying to convince her otherwise, but she has it in her head that she is a nobody, even though she is everything to Finn.

She struggles with self-worth and confidence, and every chance Finn has, he is building her up and showing her how amazing she truly is. I am incredibly proud of the man he has become.

And he is a man now. Looking at him, I can barely believe my eyes. He isn't my little buddy anymore. Finn is every bit a man. He stands at six foot two, and all the football he has played during high school has given him muscles upon muscles.

His team went to state and won, and Finn had been scouted to play for one of the A grade teams, but he turned down the offer. He told me football wasn't his dream, and that was good enough for me.

"Yeah, okay, I get it. What if we just have a little party? Like, just a couple of us? Your close friends and whatever piece Weston is bagging at the moment?" I suggest.

One side of Finn's mouth lifts. "Okay, sounds good. I'll tell Wes." Then he gets up and clears our plates off the table.

"Dishwasher's nearly full; just pop the plates in and start it. I'll do the other stuff by hand," I call out after him.

FINN'S BIRTHDAY OFFICIALLY STARTS IN TWENTY MINUTES. I SET my alarm for five A.M. before I went to bed last night so I could wake him up the second he was born eighteen-years-ago.

I creep out to the kitchen and grab the ingredients to make a quick mug cake in the microwave. When it's done, I pop a candle in the center and light it up then tiptoe to Finn's room. Twisting the door handle, I push it open as quiet as possible, then place the mug cake on his bedside table.

He's out cold. And I can't help but stand there and just stare at him for a full minute like the biggest creeper in the world. But I can't help it. He's gown into this incredible human being and somehow, I'm the one standing here watching it happen. I get to be the one to call him my son.

Emotion clogs my throat as a wave of grief crashes over me. Jacq should be here right now. She should be wishing him a happy birthday and giving him motherly advise that I could never come up with even on my best day.

I choke on a sob as I run out of Finn's room and lock myself in the bathroom. Gripping the counter, I take a few deep breaths and get myself under control. I close my eyes and drop my head to the cool surface of the sink. "I miss you Jacq," I whisper into the silence.

Taking a couple more calming breaths, I turn on the faucet and wash my face. After drying off, I return to Finn's room. The candle has nearly burnt all the way out, so I take a running jump and body slam him.

He lurches awake with a startled, "What the fuck?"

"Happy Birthday!" I laugh, then grab his mug cake and hand it to him. "Quick, make a wish before the candle goes out!"

He rolls his big brown eyes, but he's smiling when he closes his eyes and blows out the candle.

Weston has brought a girl called Candy, and she is as dumb as her name sounds. She looks like a stunned mullet when Finn sweeps Nixie up in his arms and plants a kiss on her lips. "Is she, like, his girlfriend or something?" she asks.

I look at her and realize she is truly confused. "They've only been together for the last two years. So, yeah, she's his girlfriend."

Her eyes widen at my response. "But, like, who is she?"

I give her the stink eye. "His girlfriend. I just told you that."

She shakes her head and laughs. "No, I mean, like, who *is* she? She's a nobody. How did she score a hottie like Finn?"

And that's when I show her the door, Weston right behind me, telling her there is no need to call him later; he is done.

Weston's as protective of Nixie as Finn and I are. I'm actually shocked that he brought that girl to Finn's birthday celebration. "What the hell, Weston?" I shoot at him as soon as I close the door behind his date.

He shrugs. "She gives great head." He smirks.

I narrow my eyes on him. "Always with the oversharing. Why?" I whine.

Weston throws his head back, laughing, then hooks his arm around my shoulder and steers me back into the living room where Luke, one of the boys' friends from school, Finn, and Nixie are digging into the pizzas I made upon Finn's request. "Come on, you know you love it," he says as we walk.

"I really don't," I mutter. But I kind of do. I'm used to it. Weston has always been that way. I'm pretty sure I know more about his adventurous sex life than Finn does.

"Where do you find these skanks anyway?" I ask him.

He shrugs again. "What can I say, I'm a chick magnet."

I laugh this time. "You're so full of yourself."

"Would you like to be full of me, Tory?" he says while bouncing his brows.

I start choking on my slice of pizza, and Finn's head shoots up from his plate. "Dude! Stop hitting on my mom!"

Nixie and Luke start laughing. "I think it would take more than Wes' corny lines to get inside Tory's pants, baby. I don't think you've got anything to worry about," Nixie reassures Finn.

Weston grabs his heart. "I am wounded. You have wounded me, Nix. My lines have gotten me into many a fine woman's pants."

Finn's eyes narrow. "Yeah, well, keep your lines for the women who aren't my mom."

Weston rolls his eyes. "It's not my fault your mom's the definition of a MILF."

Finn is off the couch and on top of Weston with his fist raised and ready to punch him in the face when Weston pulls a move I've never seen before and has Finn flat on his back and pinned to the ground beneath him. "Dude, this isn't news to you," he says to Finn.

"Doesn't mean I have to like it," Finn spits back.

I have no idea what is going on between them, but the playful atmosphere that usually surrounds these kinds of goings on has vanished, and the air is thick with tension. "Okay, boys, that's enough for tonight. Weston, get off my boy, and let's finish eating. I'm hungry."

Weston pushes up to his feet and holds his hand out to Finn who takes it reluctantly. "We good?" he asks as Finn stands.

Finn nods and grumbles, "Always."

They do some manly handshake hug thing, and not five minutes later, it's like it had never happened.

Boys. I will never understand them.

I HAVEN'T DATED MUCH OVER THE YEARS, PREFERRING THE company of my vibrator. Finn has been my priority and getting involved with someone would have split my focus. I wasn't prepared to do that—until now.

Finn is now eighteen and spending less and less time at home. And I'm getting lonely.

"V, I haven't had sex in over a year," I confess sadly over a glass of wine on my back porch. And even then, it had been a one-night stand with a hottie who came into the shop at closing one night. He'd asked me out for drinks since I was almost finished, and I agreed. Finn was out for the night with Weston, doing God knows what—I don't even remember any more.

Somehow, drinks had turned into hot, sweaty sex against the wall out in the back of the bar. I'm not going to lie; it was amazing. But I'd never do it again. I'm just not cut out for one-nighters.

Vera's loud snort pulls me from memory lane. "Ha! I haven't had sex in, like, three years," she retorts.

"That kinda makes me feel a little better," I admit.

Vera raises a brow. "It shouldn't. I'm not a twenty-eight-year-old hottie who still has perky tits. You have no excuse for your lack of action."

I gasp. "I do too! And you've still got it, V. You should totally be out there picking up."

She scoffs, takes another hearty swig of her wine, and

levels me with her narrowed eyes. "Listen here, girly, I've got thirteen years on you, and you're tellin' me I should be out there picking up? Look at yourself. Why are you not out there picking up?"

I shrug. "I hear forty is the new twenty."

Vera snorts. "Lies. It's all lies."

We both start cackling, then Finn and Weston open the sliding door and poke their heads out. "What's so funny?" Finn asks.

Finishing the last of my wine, I reach for the bottle to refill my glass and realize it's empty. "Any left in your bottle?" I ask Vera. We know by now that we need a bottle each for evenings such as these.

Vera's drunken frown turns to me. "I'm out."

We turn our focus to the boys who are still standing in the open sliding door. "Wine! We need more wine!" I demand.

Finn crosses his arms over his broad chest. "Really? You sure about that? Walk to me in a straight line, and I'll get you more wine."

"I'm drowning my sorrows," I cry.

His expression morphs to one of concern, his brows furrowing together as he stares at me. "Why? What's wrong?"

If I hadn't just consumed a whole bottle of wine in less than an hour, I would have kept my mouth shut. But I have just consumed a whole bottle of wine, so I tell him, "My sex life is non-existent. It's depressing. My vagina hasn't seen a real live penis in over a year."

Finn's face morphs again but, this time, into revulsion. "Uh! Stop talking. I'll get more wine if you just stop talking.

And never say the word penis or vagina in front of me again."

"Penis, penis, penis," I chant then begin to sing, "Big ones, small ones, some as big as your head!"

Weston is bent over at the waist, laughing, and Finn is turning green. He spins on his heel and heads back inside. "I'm getting the wine! Now shut up!"

"Thank you!" I call after him.

Weston takes the opportunity to offer my vagina his services. "I've got a damn fine penis that would be more than happy to meet your vagina, Tory," he says with mirth, trying desperately to hold back his laughter.

Vera picks up the spare chair cushion and throws it at her horndog son. "Weston Banks, you dirty little bastard!" she chides.

Weston continues to laugh until Finn returns with a chilled bottle of wine and fills my glass for me then Vera's. "If you weren't my mom, I'd probably find this funny. But you are. And I don't ever want to hear about your sex life again," he says with a stern expression covering his handsome face.

I wave my hand at him. "I didn't want to know about yours, but that didn't stop you from having sex on my Netflix couch, did it?"

His face turns beet red, then his eyes narrow. "Keep it up and I'm cutting you off," he threatens, holding the wine bottle out over the garden, poised to pour.

"You're such a buzz kill," I complain.

I regret the whole conversation the next morning.

I also regret the amount of wine I consumed. I have the hangover from hell, and when I finally stumble out of my room at ten AM, Finn laughs in my face, making my head pound so hard I think my eyes are going to explode.

Chapter Nine

Victoria

Two Years Ago . . .

I'm going on an actual date. Like, a real one with a man, not my vibrator.

Nervous doesn't begin to describe how I'm feeling. My stomach's in knots, and the date isn't even until Saturday night. A whole two days away.

When I finish my shift, I head home to shower and pop on a fresh pair of jeans, a loose tank, and a pair of sandals. I've decided a new outfit would make me feel better about my upcoming date.

As I step up to the front door and place my hand on the handle, I hear the back door slide open. Glancing over my shoulder, I catch Weston strolling in. "Bad time?" he asks when he spots me at the front door.

"Uh, kinda. I'm just heading out. Late-night shopping," I explain.

His face brightens. "I'll come with. I need some new

jeans. And I hate shopping on my own; I feel like such a loser."

"You are a loser."

Shaking his head, he lifts a brow. "Lame insult, Tory. You can do better than that."

I look up to the left and gnaw on the corner of my lip, trying to come up with something. But before I can, Weston darts forward, grabs me by the waist, and throws me over his shoulder.

I scream and laugh. "What are you doing?"

"You were taking too long," he says as he opens the front door, stepping out and closing it behind him, all while I am still hanging over his shoulder.

Looking down, I unconsciously lick my lips. He has a damn fine ass. I have a sudden urge to reach out and slap it. So I do.

Weston chuckles as he strides toward his truck parked in his driveway. "Keep that up, and I'll be returning the favor, Tory."

I swallow—hard. Because the idea of Weston spanking me should not send a shiver down my spine.

Once he reaches the passenger door of his truck, he shifts me and slowly lowers me down the front of his body until my feet hit the ground. Looking up into his eyes, I swallow again. Licking my lips, I mumble, "I guess you're driving then, huh?"

His lips quirk in a grin. "I'll drive you wherever you want to go, Tory."

The look in his eyes now has my heart rate picking up speed. I spin around and grab the door handle, yanking it open. "The plaza will be fine," I say over my shoulder as I climb up into the cab.

Latching my seatbelt, I fix my eyes on my hands locked together in my lap. He should not be able to evoke such responses from me. He's Weston. What is wrong with me?

Weston turns the radio up as he drives. "Hands to Myself" comes on, and I feel Weston's eyes on the side of my face. Glancing at him from the corner of my eye, I catch the grin on his face right before he reaches over and starts poking me in the ribs.

I squeal and jump in my seat, plastering myself against the door as he sings out at the top of his lungs, "Can't keep my hands to myself."

Laughter bubbles up from my stomach, and I collapse into myself as I struggle to breath. He keeps singing along to the song with a huge grin on his handsome face, his eyes flicking over to me every other second they aren't on the road.

When the song ends, he takes a mock bow. "Thank you, thank you, please hold your applause."

"You're such a dick." I laugh.

"Took that miserable look off your face, though, didn't it?"

I look over at him watching me while stopped at a red light. I smile softly. "It did."

He continues to sing along at the top of his lungs to every song on the radio for the remainder of the drive to the shopping center. There is even a little old school Bieber in there. And I continue to laugh, my stomach in a whole different kind of knot by the time he parks the car and turns off the ignition.

Grinning at him, I unfasten my seatbelt. "Come on, Bono. I've gotta get a new outfit for my hot date."

His beaming smile drops from his face at my words, and

his gaze sharpens. But he doesn't say anything as he slides out of his seat and slams his door shut.

Shit. Why did I say that?

I jump down from my side of the truck and jog to catch up with him. As soon as I'm by his side, he clicks the button on his keys, locking his truck, then shoves them in his pocket.

"Weston, wait up," I huff.

He slows his pace minutely and glares down at me. "Why? So you can get my opinion of your hot new outfit for another guy? No thanks."

"If I had known you would act like a spoiled brat, I would have just come on my own," I grumble then turn around, heading for the other entrance. "I'll take an Uber home. Thanks for the lift," I call over my shoulder.

I half expect him to come after me. He doesn't.

My shoulders slump at the sound of approaching footsteps, but he returns to his truck and pulls out of the parking lot, not even sparing me a glance as he drives past.

The last thing I feel like doing now is shopping, so I pull my phone out of my back pocket and order a ride. Ten minutes later, I am on my way back home.

Weston's truck is nowhere to be seen as I climb out of the small car and stride toward my front door.

I spend the rest of the night eating a tub of cookies-and-cream ice cream while binge-watching *Vampire Diaries* on Netflix. Say what you like about that show, but Damon is hot.

Saturday night, I sit on my couch in a simple pair of black skinny jeans matched with a loose-fitting, white, racerback tank and a pair of silver sandals on my feet. I've left my long ash blonde hair down, just pulling a few strands back away from my face and pinning them together at the back.

Finn comes out of his room dressed up as well. "Lookin' good, Mom. Where did you say you found this guy?" he asks a little too casually.

I raise a brow. "He's Jane's brother. Why?"

He shrugs, feigning nonchalance. "No reason."

When a knock sounds from the front door, Finn takes off to answer it before I even get up off the couch.

He leans against the open doorframe and crosses his arms over his chest as he looks Brian up and down. Then, to my horror, Weston steps up behind Finn. I hadn't even seen him come in. He glares at Brian. "What do you want?" he asks.

I have just died of embarrassment. I jump up and run to the door, but the boys are blocking me. "Move!" I demand.

Both Finn and Weston glance at me over their shoulders and shake their heads. "Do you mind? We're kinda in the middle of something here," Finn says.

I cross my arms. "Like what?"

"Intimidating him, what does it look like?" He roll of his eyes, then he turns his focus back to Brian. "I'm going to need your full name, phone number, criminal record, and employment status before I allow you to date my mom."

I get up on my tippy toes to see Brian over their shoulders. He looks relaxed and not at all offended by the boys' behavior. He reaches out and shakes Finn's hand. "I'm Brian Adrian Morelli. I don't have a criminal record that I'm aware of, there might be a parking ticket or two in my history, if that counts. I work for my family company, Morelli Motor Group. But if you want my number, you'll have to buy me a drink first," he says with a little wink in Finn's direction.

Finn grins and looks back at me. "He passed; you can go now. Be back by eleven." He kisses me on the forehead and strides back down the hall to his room.

Weston, however, is still solid as a brick wall, glaring at Brian like he wants to rip his throat out. I elbow him in the ribs. "Don't you have somewhere you're meant to be?" I growl.

His glare shifts from Brian to me, and I swallow. He has the intimidation thing down pat. Then, without a word, he stalks away. *Well, that was intense.* I clear my throat and smile at Brian. "Sorry about that."

He shrugs. "No worries. You ready?"

Nodding, I turn back to see Weston leaning his back against the kitchen counter, arms crossed, that angry glare still plastered on his face. I give him a small finger wave goodbye and take Brian's outstretched hand, following him out to his car.

Chapter Ten

Victoria

My date last night with Brian was, unfortunately, *not* everything I imagined it would be.

The whole time, all I could think about was Weston and his obvious disapproval. No matter how charming Brian was, my mind kept drifting back to the scowl on Weston's face when I left.

I couldn't focus on anything Brian said, and he knew it too. He came right out and asked if something was wrong because I seemed distracted. I told him I was just really tired, that I hadn't been sleeping very well, and he bought it. Thankfully.

But the surprising thing is, my disinterest hasn't deterred him, because he just texted me.

BRIAN: I feel like last night could have gone so much better. And I'm really into you Tory. So, I'm asking for a do-over. When you're not feeling so run down, of course.

I swallow, not sure how to respond. I stare at my cell for a good thirty minutes before deciding I owe it to him, and myself to give this a real chance. He is super nice, and the way he handled Finn with both respect and humor scored him mega points. Plus, he's pretty cute in a Logan Lerman in that Nazi hunters show, kind of way.

Gnawing on my bottom lip, I type out a response.

TORY: Thank you, I'd like that. How about next weekend? Friday night?

His response is immediate. And I feel like a bit of a dick for taking so long to get back to him in the first place. But just like that, I have another date planned.

Still unsure how I feel about it, I sigh and my stomach rumbles. It's almost noon and I haven't eaten yet. I drag my butt off the couch and make my way to the kitchen.

I'm in the middle of making a sandwich when I hear the back sliding door open then close. I poke my head around the corner and see Weston walking in. "Finn's not home," I tell him while chewing on a piece of cheese.

I expect him to turn around and leave, but he just keeps coming toward me. I shrug and go back to making my lunch.

When I turn around, Weston is right behind me. I startle and almost drop my plate, but he catches it. "What are you doing?" I ask, hand over my pounding heart.

He takes a step closer and puts the plate with my sandwich on the counter behind me. His eyes are intent on mine, and I have a really bad feeling. I swallow hard as he takes another step closer, forcing me to shuffle back until my butt hits the cupboard behind me.

Weston moves closer still, giving me nowhere to go. I

have to tilt my face up to meet his gaze. *He's so close.* "Weston, wha—what are you doing?" I stutter.

His firm body is pressed against me, and I can feel tension radiating off him in waves. "Don't go out with him again," he clips out, his jaw clenching and unclenching as if he's struggling with his control.

I frown. What business is it of his? "Excuse me?" I snap.

His intense stare flicks to my lips for a brief moment, then returns to my eyes again. "Don't go."

I huff my annoyance and lift my hands to push him away, but he doesn't budge. His body is rigid, unmoving. "Why?" I finally ask when it's clear I can't move him.

"I don't want you to," he says as if that makes perfect sense.

I shake my head. "What's going on here? Why don't you want me to go? Is Brian some kind of creeper or something?"

Weston lifts one shoulder in a shrug. "Don't know."

Sighing, I click my tongue. "Okay," I draw the word out. "So what's the problem then?"

My eyes widen as Weston slowly lowers his face and I arch my back, moving my mouth out of reach from his, and he sighs. "Tory," he breathes my name, and flows over my lips in a gentle caress.

I search his eyes. "Weston, I don't understand."

His heart hammers under my palm as he closes his eyes and presses his forehead to mine. "You never have. I'm beginning to think you never will," he murmurs.

And just like that, it hits me square in the chest. These last few years, I've been trying to pretend that all the times Weston has flirted with me, it was just good-natured and nothing serious. Certainly nothing worth worrying about.

It's just his personality. But right now, in this moment, I know. I've only been fooling myself.

Tears I don't expect prickle my eyes. "No, Weston, I can't. *You* can't," I plead.

His broad chest shudders as he releases a deep breath. My eyelids shutter closed as he brushes a feather-light kiss to the top of my head, his lips lingering a second, then two… and then he's gone.

He leaves me standing alone in my kitchen, wondering if I just imagined this whole thing.

Pushing my fingers into my hair, I want to scream. He's just ruined everything. The whole dynamic of our little group is never going to be the same. It can't be.

I'm about to turn thirty. And he just hit twenty a matter weeks ago. He's my son's best friend. Nothing about what just happened is okay. But I don't know what to do about it.

A WEEK PASSES, AND WESTON HASN'T BEEN AROUND LIKE usual.

"Hey, you seen Wes lately?" Finn asks me one afternoon when he gets home from work.

"What? No. Why would I?" I answer, then clamp my mouth closed. *What is wrong with me?* Finn eyes me with suspicion but doesn't push the issue.

The boys have beers together after work most afternoons, and we all eat together at least once a week. But Weston didn't show this week. I didn't ask after him and Vera didn't offer up any explanation for his absence. To miss one here or there isn't a big deal, but I have a feeling, deep in my gut, he's not going to show for a while.

A heavy weight settles in my chest at the thought of him essentially deserting us. He's an important part of our lives here in Shiloh Springs. Has been since day one. I can't even begin to imagine not seeing him most days, if not every one.

By Thursday night, I know I can't go out with Brian again. So, I take the cowards way out, and text him. I feel horrible not giving him so much as an explanation, but my head is such a mess right now. I can't think straight. A do-over isn't going to go any better than our first date.

Later that night, I lay in my bed staring at my ceiling as my mind runs in circles. Did I cancel on Brian because Weston didn't want me to go out with him again? Was it because *I* didn't want to? Or was it because I'm terrified of what starting a relationship with someone, anyone, will do to me and Finn's relationship?

It's been just the two of us for so long. I can't imagine bringing someone else into our space, our home. Not everyone gets our dynamic. We're not exactly a typical mother and son. And I don't know how I feel explaining us to someone outside of our bubble.

First world introvert problems. I snort and shake my head at myself, then roll to my side and close my eyes, praying my brain will take pity on me and stop bombarding me with thoughts that are far from conducive to sleep.

It takes some time, but finally my thoughts slow, and I drift into a restless slumber.

Two days later, and I still can't decide which it is.

But I can't stop thinking back to last weekend, Weston backing me against the kitchen counter, and making his feelings abundantly clear. It doesn't matter what I do to try to distract myself; it, no *he,* is constantly on my mind.

"Yo, Tor, you okay girl? You've been off lately," Jane, my assistant manager, asks on Monday morning when I can't get the cash float to balance and keep starting over.

I grit my teeth in frustration. This normally takes me less than five minutes, but I've already been at it for ten already, and it still isn't adding up. I close the register and turn to Jane. "No. No, I'm not okay, Jane. And I don't know how to fix it."

Jane quirks her pierced brow. "What's got you so twisted up? I've never seen you like this. You're not screwed up over Brian, are you? 'Cause I've already set him up with someone else."

A humorless laugh erupts from my lips. "No, not Brian, and sorry about that, by the way."

She shrugs it off. "No sweat, dude. You guys didn't mesh; not a problem. That's what dating is for. You like 'em, or you don't. So, if it's not Brian messing with your head, then who?"

"Weston, of all people," I say then blow my bangs out of my eyes.

Her eyes widen comically. "Weston? As in Finn's hot friend?"

I roll my eyes. "Yes, as in Finn's *best* friend. As in totally-untouchable-for-so-many-reasons, Weston."

Jane snorts. "Why's he untouchable? I'd like to touch him. A lot," she says, waggling her eyebrows.

I shove her shoulder. "Dude eww, he only just turned twenty. He's a baby." I gesture to myself. "And I'm gearing up to hit thirty."

She shrugs. "So what? I'd do him. Ten years is nothing. My parents are, like, fifteen years apart."

My eyes bug out now. "Really?" I squeak.

Jane laughs. "Yeah, it worked for them. Mind you, Grandpa wasn't real happy about it when his little girl started dating a grown man. But he got over it when he realized they were perfect for each other."

I huff. "That's different. Your dad is older than your mom. That's totally fine. I however, have no plans to enter Cougar Town."

"Cougar Town?" Jane asks, furrowing her brows. "Like the TV show?"

Shaking my head, I roll my eyes at her. "No, I mean, I'm not into younger men—let alone ten years younger and my son's best friend."

Jane shrugs. "Your loss. He's hot." Then she turns around to go open the door to the shop.

"Thanks, good talk, so helpful," I call out after her.

"You're welcome," she calls back as she weaves through clothing racks, heading for the entrance to open the doors for customers.

Finally, I manage to get the register to balance just as the first customer of the day enters the store. "I'm going out back to work on next week's roster," I tell Jane then disappear into my office for the rest of the day.

I DON'T SLEEP WELL THAT NIGHT—AND HAVEN'T ANY NIGHT before it since Weston ruined everything. Each night, I fall into my bed, exhausted and praying I won't be consumed by the same dream I've been having since he cornered me in my kitchen.

I wake in the middle of the night in a sweaty, tangled mess in my sheets, panting with an empty ache between my legs. I dream of that day, standing in my kitchen, Weston's hard body pressed against me. But in my dreams, I don't pull away. I don't stop him.

He presses his soft, full lips to mine. His tongue caressing mine, rhythmically stroking, teasing. I arch my back, pressing my breasts into his chest, and he groans into my mouth as he grinds his pelvis into mine, making me moan his name.

And then I wake up.

Wanting. Craving. Needing.

But I can never have him.

He is my son's best friend.

He is *my* best friend's son.

He is forbidden.

Chapter Eleven

Victoria

One Year Ago . . .

Finn is moving out and I'm a mess.

"Stop crying. I'm not going far. Nix and I will be eating here, like, every night. She's not a very good cook. Don't tell her I said that, though," Finn says, wrapping one of his long arms around my shoulders.

"You better," I mumble as I wipe my nose.

Finn smirks down at me. "I'm really only moving out so you don't have to listen to Nix screaming out my name when I'm rocking her world between the sheets," he says with a waggle of his brows.

I dry heave. "Eww Finn!"

He laughs and runs away from my swatting hands. "What? You hate it when you can hear us, I'm doing you a solid."

"I thought discussing your sex life was in the little black

box that also holds all discussions about my sex life and is hidden at the back of the hallway closet?"

"It is," he says. "The difference is, I actually have a sex life, and—" he pats the top of my head and smirks, "—you don't."

My jaw drops. "I do too."

Finn puts his hands on his hips, then levels me with a glare. "Oh, really? You know if it's battery-operated, it doesn't count. When was the last time you actually got laid?"

My eyes widen. "Hey! What happened to the little black box?"

He lifts one shoulder in a slight shrug. "I'm opening the box, but just for a minute."

"Well, I'm closing it again!" I snap.

He shakes his head and holds an imaginary box above him. "You can't. I'm taller than you, and you can't reach it. So spill."

I suddenly feel very small under his scrutinizing gaze. "It's been a while, but now that you're moving out, I might go out and get me some." I am proud of my answer, but Finn doesn't buy it.

"How long is a while?" he pushes.

"Jesus, Finn, I don't know. It's not like I marked it on my calendar," I snap at him, already way over this conversation and more than ready to help him put the last couple of boxes in the bed of his truck.

He sighs and brings his hands down on my shoulders. "I'm just worried about you, is all."

I raise a brow. "You're worried I'm not having enough sex? That's a bit weird, Finn."

He smirks. "We're weird, remember? It's what we do."

I roll my eyes and grumble, "Doesn't mean we discuss our sex lives."

He huffs. "Why are you being so difficult?"

"Why are you asking me about my sex life?" I shoot back.

"Because you're young, Mom. You should be out having fun. Living your life." He sighs again then continues, "If it weren't for me, you'd probably be married by now—"

My hand shoots up and covers his mouth. "Stop right there. I wouldn't change anything, Finn. I don't regret our life. I don't regret my choices. Do you understand? I don't ever want you to feel guilty about anything that has to do with me. I've had an amazing life... *because* of you." Tears prickle my eyes again as I reach up and cup his stubbled cheek. "You're my little buddy. Well"—I frown—"you're not so little anymore, but you're still my buddy."

Finn's eyes shine with unshed tears. "I just feel like I've held you back."

I shake my head and smile. "Dude, you are so wrong."

Finn's big arms wrap around me and pull me close. "I love you, Mom. You gave me a good life. A happy life. When I thought I'd never be happy again, you gave me that." He sighs heavily. "This is just another stage for us. I'm not moving on, I'm just moving out. You're still my mom, and I'm still going to need you."

I lose the battle with my tears and let them fall. I mush my face into his chest and sob. "You're the best thing that ever happened to me, Finn. Being your mom has been the greatest gift to me."

We stand there, holding on to everything that we have been through together, getting ready to let it go and start a new chapter, when Weston bursts through the front door, interrupting our emotional moment.

"Uh, shit, sorry. I'll wait out front," he says to Finn.

Weston hasn't been around much since that day in my kitchen. I rarely see him anymore, and if I do, I find a way to excuse myself without making a big deal of it. I can't stand being around him, my body reacting in a way that it shouldn't. And that can't happen.

I squeeze Finn extra tight. "You better get going, I'll make sure I've got something really good ready for dinner tonight."

Finn bites his lip. "About that... I know I said we'd be eating here, like, every night—but not tonight. We kinda wanted to christen our first place together tonight."

My eyes light with realization. "Oh! Well, okay. Tomorrow night, then?"

A contented smile fills Finn's face. "Tomorrow night. Bye, Mom." He kisses my forehead, lets me go, then walks out the front door.

I go to my bedroom and cry.

It's dark outside when I open my swollen eyes. I must have fallen asleep crying.

I huff and try to roll over, but a solid weight is laying across my stomach, pinning me in place.

Before I can freak out, a deep, sleepy male voice murmurs, "Stop moving. Sleeping."

A shrill scream leaves my lungs, and the weight disappears as I launch myself from my bed, touching my bedside lamp on my way to illuminate the room, only to turn around and find a sleep-mussed Weston in my bed.

My eyes grow so wide they nearly fall out of my head.

Weston's tattooed arm moves up to cover his eyes. "Too bright," he mutters.

"What the hell are you doing in my bed, Weston?" I screech.

His mouth opens then closes with a deep yawn. "Finn asked me to come check on you after I helped move all his shit this afternoon. I came over, let myself in, you were sleeping, I was tired, so I joined you." He shrugs like it is no big deal for him to be snuggled up in my bed.

"Are you insane? You live next door. Why couldn't you go home to sleep?" I'm pacing back and forth at the foot of my bed now, waiting for his answer.

Weston sits up abruptly, reaches for my hand, and yanks me back into the bed on top of him. I squirm and struggle to get back to my feet, but he is too strong and holds me in place with his arms wrapped around my middle.

"Let me go, Weston! This is not appropriate!" I cry.

"Fuck appropriate, Tory. I'm sick of appropriate. And while we're at it, I'm sick of you avoiding me like I'm the fucking plague," he fumes.

My struggles cease at the tone of his voice. I've never heard him speak like that before. "It's not like that—"

"Yes, Tory, it's exactly like that. You've been avoiding me since that day in your kitchen. And I'm sick of it. I miss your face. I miss your voice. I miss *you*, Tor. So, when I came in here and saw your tear-stained cheeks, I couldn't stop myself from climbing in behind you and holding you for a little while." His voice has softened, as has his hold around me.

I don't know what to say. Today has been far too emotional already. I can't do this. Not right now. Not ever, really. But I can't stop myself from soaking up the comfort he offers, if only for a few moments.

His large, calloused hands sweep up and down my back, soothing me, and I let him.

A few minutes pass with not a word spoken between us. I take a deep breath and push myself up so I can look down at his face. He isn't the ten-year-old boy who befriended my son anymore. He is a man—a very attractive man who could have any woman he pleases, yet here he is, in my bed.

"Why?" I ask softly, needing to understand.

Weston's hands come up to tuck my hair away from my face and cup my cheeks. "You are the most selfless woman I have ever known. You've put Finn's needs ahead of your own for as long as I have known you two. But it's not just Finn's needs you put first, it's mine too."

One of his hands slides down and around my neck, coming to rest over my heart. "Your heart beats for those around you." He pauses, licking his lips. "And my heart... it beats for *you*."

My eyes sting, nobody has ever spoken to me like that. As my tears begin to fall, Weston lifts himself up on his elbows, bringing his face closer to mine until he brushes a feather-light kiss to each of my cheeks, then my lips. It's soft. It's tender. And it speaks so loudly of his feelings for me. It makes my tears fall harder.

I'VE BEEN KEEPING MY FEELINGS ON LOCKDOWN FOR FAR TOO long.

I can't keep doing it. Tory is in my arms, and I don't see my best friend's mom. I see the woman I want, the woman I need. And for the first time ever, I see my feelings reflected in her eyes.

Closing the small space between our bodies, I cup her cheek and stroke the pad of my thumb over her plump bottom lip. How many times have I wanted to touch that lip? To bite it? To lick it? To suck on it?

She releases a strangled groan. "Weston." My name on her lips, that soft breathy moan does something to my rational thoughts, and I close the distance between our mouths and do all the things I've been aching to do to that lip.

Tory's hands slide up into my hair as she clings to me. I pull away just a whisper. "Don't make me keep waiting, Tory," I breathe.

She shudders under my palm, then she closes her eyes so tightly her nose crinkles. "Weston, this is so wrong."

Smoothing my thumb over her lip again, making her eyes flash open, I grin at her. "But what if it's right?"

Victoria

When he draws back, a deep tormented sob tears from my throat. "I'm so sorry, Weston. I can't do this." Before he can stop me, I slide from the bed and lock myself in my adjoining bathroom.

I can hear him trying to open the door, but I ignore him.

"Let me in, Tory. We need to talk," he growls through the door.

I fight to gain my composure. "You have to go, Weston. Please, you need to leave."

"Goddamn it, Tory, when are you going realize I'm not a boy anymore?" He emphasizes his words with a pound of his fist against the door.

I know he is no longer a boy. I've known it for a long time. But that doesn't change the fact that he is still my son's best friend. I place my hand against the cool timber separating us. "I know, Weston. I do." I take a shuddering breath. "But it's so much more complicated than that."

"Then explain it to me," he pleads. "I've just laid myself out to you, Tory. You owe me that much."

Chewing on my lip, I know opening the door will make this so much harder. I can't look at him right now, not when I am feeling so weak, so vulnerable, so alone. "You haven't been a boy to me for a long time, Weston. That's why I've avoided you. This can't happen, you and me. You're Finn's best friend. It wouldn't be right."

"Why? Because of what people would say? Fuck what anyone else thinks. This is about you and me, Tor. Nobody else. Finn would get over it, I guarantee it. Just open the door, *please.*"

My lip is raw from my gnawing teeth, but I can't stop. I need the pain to distract me, to keep me from opening the door and going to him. I can feel his torment through the and it eats at my soul.

"I'm sorry, Weston." And that's all I can say. I'm devastated, and I'm ashamed.

Eventually, I hear him leave, but I stay in the bathroom for a long time after. I make myself a hot bath and slide into its steamy depths, hoping to calm my mind enough to find some clarity in all this.

In the weeks that follow, I never see Weston. Now that Finn has moved out, there is no reason for him to randomly pop in, even though he still lives next door. I get the distinct impression that he—like I had done to him—is avoiding me.

I don't blame him. In all honesty, I don't know what I'll do if I see him, so it is best that doesn't happen.

My mind, as well as my heart, has been twisted in knots since Finn moved out.

I rub at my chest, trying to relieve the ache that settled there the day he left. But it doesn't work. I miss him fiercely, even though, true to his word, he and Nixie do eat dinner at my place nearly every night.

But things have changed, and I need to find a way to adjust to our new dynamic.

I have to figure out who I am, outside of being Finn's mom.

And that might just be the hardest thing of all.

Chapter Twelve

Victoria

Nine Months Ago . . .

"Momma, I'm home!" Finn sings out as he swings the front door open.

I laugh and glance up to the clock on the kitchen wall. "Dinner isn't ready yet, you guys are super early. What's the occasion?"

Finn is positively beaming, and Nixie is glowing. I raise a brow in suspicion. "You two better not be here to tell me I'm going to be a grandma. I'm not nearly ready for that."

They laugh as they continue their approach, and my eyes flick back and forth between them. Something is up. And I'm dying to know what. "I'm not getting any younger here. If you're going to age me twenty years in one afternoon, I'd prefer you did it quickly."

Nixie grins. "We're just waiting on Wes, then we'll tell you our big news."

My heart leaps into my throat. "Weston is coming over? Like, here? Now?"

Finn's expression morphs from elation to caution instantly. "Yeah, why?"

I busy my hands, wiping down the already clean counter tops around me. "No reason. Must be big news if you need us both here for it."

Before Finn can push the issue, the back door slides open, and a freshly showered Weston walks in. "Alright, dude, if it's a boy, you have to call him Weston Junior. I'm still working on a female twist to my name, but I'm sure I'll figure something out if it turns out you have Barbie balls."

Nixie bursts out laughing while Finn glares at his best friend. "Barbie balls?" he asks, clearly offended. "My first born will most definitely be a boy, just to prove the manliness of my nuts. But you can hold off on the female rendition for now, we're not pregnant."

I want to feel relieved by that statement, but with Weston in the room, there is no way my heart rate is going to slow down anytime soon.

Weston appears crestfallen. "So, no little Westina?"

Finn shakes his head. "I'm afraid not, bro, not right now. And with a name like Westina, not ever."

Nixie is still laughing at their exchange, and normally, I would be too. But I am still struggling to regain my equilibrium.

"I'll try to come up with something better, but it's a good back-up name," Weston says as he punches Finn in the shoulder.

That move begins a fake scuffle between the two. They are always trying to kick each other's ass. It must be a guy thing. Nixie and I get out of the way and wait for them to finish.

By the time they're done, they're both sweaty and disheveled. "Have you proved your masculinity yet, baby?" Nixie asks when Finn drapes his arm over her shoulder and drops a kiss on the top of her head.

My heart aches, they are so perfect for each other. Seeing them together like this always makes me simultaneously happy and a wee bit envious. I want that for myself. Unconsciously, my gazes flick over to Weston, who's also watching Finn and Nixie's exchange.

When his gaze moves over to me, I quickly avert my eyes and clear my throat. "So, what's the big news then?"

Finn looks me in the eye. "We're getting married."

And just like that, my heart stops beating.

My boy is getting married.

It isn't that I'm not happy for him. I am. Ecstatically so.

But I feel like I've only just started getting used to him not living with me, and now he is going to be a married man.

Everything is changing so quickly. Everything except me.

I'm still the same. I work the same job, live in the same house, do the same things, day in and day out. I'm living the same life I started the day Finn and I moved to Shiloh Springs.

I need to move forward. But I don't know how.

Weston's touch on my forearm jerks me from my selfish thoughts. "You okay, Tor?"

His hand lingers on my arm, my eyes locked on the point of contact, my skin burning where we touch.

"Tory?" he whispers, making my eyes move to his. The concern shining back at me snaps me out of my tailspin.

I pull away from his touch. It takes more effort than I'd

like to admit, but I do it. "Yeah, I'm fine. I just had myself all worked up to become a grandmother." A shaky laugh slips past my lips. "Thank God that's not on tonight's agenda!"

Finn and Nixie laugh at my lame attempt to shift the focus back to them, but Weston doesn't buy it, and keeps a watchful eye on me. It's unnerving. *He's* unnerving. I clear my throat. "So, why'd you need us both for the big announcement?"

"Because you guys are the two most important people in our lives," Finn explains with a *duh* expression on his face.

THAT NIGHT, I LIE IN MY BED, TRYING DESPERATELY TO THINK of a way out of the funk I've found myself in. Then, as if she is lying right next to me, I hear Jacq's voice. *This is your calling, Tory. How long have you been hiding this little talent of yours? You absolutely have to make something of this.*

I bolt upright in my bed, flicking on my lamp and looking around the room, sure she is in there with me. But of course she isn't. I've had many moments like this over the years since she left us. It makes me believe that she is still here, maybe not physically, but her spirit is never far from us.

And she has shown me the way, yet again.

I know what I need to do. A weight lifts off my chest, and for the first time in months, I'm able to breathe easy.

The next morning, I hand in my notice to the head office, giving them one month to replace me. Training someone to take over a position I've held for over a decade will take a couple of weeks, I don't want to screw them over.

One month will also give me time to get things in order for my next chapter.

As soon as I get home, I pull out my laptop and start ordering supplies. I'm giddy with excitement that I haven't felt in God knows how long.

Chapter Thirteen

Victoria

Six Months Ago . . .

"So, Finn and I have been talking about our bridal party, and as you know, I don't really have many girlfriends, so I was hoping you would be my maid of honor?" Nixie says, nervously picking at her hot-pink nail polish.

To say I'm shocked is an understatement. Noticing my expression, she hurries to continue. "Please don't say no. My lack of girlfriends isn't the only reason I want you, Tory." She glances down at her nails again then takes a deep breath. "You have been my confidant and biggest supporter, besides Finn, throughout our whole relationship. You're one of my best friends, and I don't care how lame that sounds."

Tears prick my eyes. That is the sweetest thing anyone has ever said to me. "I'd love to be your lame best friend slash maid of honor." I sniffle, and Nixie throws her arms around my shoulders and pulls me in for a hug. She's stronger than she looks.

When she finally releases me from her death-grip hug, I ask, "So, who else is going to be in the bridal party?"

She sits back in her seat and picks up her coffee. "Well, Weston, obviously. And I'm going to ask my cousin, Beth, to partner up with Luke."

My heart starts beating all over the place. Of course Weston would be the best man. *Stupid, stupid, stupid.* I want to bang my head on the table, but that would make my distress obvious.

So, instead of making a scene, I pick up my coffee and take a mouthful, burning my tongue in the process. I start choking as I try to spit it back into my mug. "Hot!" I pant, fanning my tongue.

Nixie bursts out laughing. "Oh my God, are you okay?"

Tears leak from the corners of my eyes, but I nod. "Ice?" I ask, and Nixie gets up to retrieve some from the freezer.

When she returns with a cup filled to the brim, I gratefully take it and pop a cube into my mouth. "So, Luke, huh?" I mutter around the ice.

Nix nods. "Yeah, he's been the boys' third wheel for years now. I mean, he's not as close to Finn as Wes, but he's always been supportive of our relationship, and he helped shut down the mean-girl movement when we were in high school."

Luke has been around a fair bit since they graduated, but I guess I haven't really noticed. I've always been too preoccupied with Weston.

And doesn't that thought cause my brain to nearly explode.

I jump under Nixie's touch on my arm. "You alright there, Tor? You look like you just swallowed that ice cube whole."

My eyes widen. "Umm, yeah—I mean, no, I didn't swallow it." I poke my tongue out, showing her the small square of ice that remains.

She tilts her head to the side. "Are you alright? You've seemed a bit distracted lately?"

Sighing, I know it's time to tell her. I've kept my new occupation a secret for the last few months, not sure if it would pan out the way I'd hoped. "Come with me," I say, then I get up and make my way down to Finn's old room.

"You haven't turned it into some creepy shrine, have you?" Nix jokes from behind me.

I laugh. "No, do you think I'm *that* crazy?"

"Well . . ." Nix trails off as she gets a good look at what I've done to the room. "Holy crap, Tory, what is all this stuff?"

"My new workshop. I quit Taylors about two months ago, and I've been designing and creating jewelry from right here," I explain as she walks around the room, her fingers gently touching some of the pieces that lay half-finished on the counter running along the wall below the window.

"These are amazing, Tory." She looks up at me, wonder in her eyes. "You made all these?"

I nod, smiling wide as pride fills my chest.

Nix shakes her head. "Why didn't you tell us?"

Shrugging, I go over to my storage unit in the corner. "I didn't know if it would work out, and I didn't want to worry Finn. But a couple of the boutiques in town have commissioned me to make pieces for them, and I'm actually doing better financially now than I was before."

When I slowly turn around and hold out my hands to Nixie, she gasps. "I made this for you. For the wedding," I explain.

"Oh, Tory, it's incredible," she gushes as she fingers the

piece gently. "I love it." Then she throws her arms around me, pulling me into another tight hug. When she pulls back, she's smiling. "Think you can make matching ones for you and Beth?"

"Of course!"

A LIGHT TAP ON THE DOOR FRAME TO MY NEWLY APPOINTED workshop startles me, making me drop the glass pearl I was threading through a thin piece of wire for my latest project. "Shit," I mutter as I turn my head to see who's so rudely interrupting me.

Weston leans against the frame, his head tilted to the side, his thickly muscled arms crossed over his wide chest, watching me.

I lick my lips and turn back to my bench, pretending to look for the errant pearl. "How long have you been standing there?" I ask over my shoulder.

"A while," he replies in a seductively deep tone.

Squeezing my eyes shut, I try desperately to remember he is my twenty-two-year-old son's best friend—a fact I've been having to remind myself of nearly every day recently.

Before I can respond, I feel the heat from his body behind me, then his arms come around my sides, gripping the edge of my work bench. "So, we're going to be partnered up for the wedding. How do you feel about that, Tor?" His voice tickles my ear as he speaks.

I have to force myself to stay still, not an easy task when my body is trying to make me lean back into the warmth of his chest and revel in his nearness. "I, uh—" I pause to steady my voice. "I'm undecided."

His chest vibrates behind me as he softly chuckles. "You know what I think? I think you're freaking out. I think you're worried you won't be able to hold back those looks you cast my way when you think nobody's watching. I think you want me every bit as much as I want you, and you're afraid."

Licking my lips, I glance up at him, hovering over my shoulder. His eyes are full of lust and a tiny bit of mirth. He's playing with me. And that pisses me the hell off. I take a steadying breath. "This isn't a game, Weston. This isn't cat and mouse, and I'm not running from you anymore."

He raises a speculative brow. "No shit, Tor. This is my life. Our life. And I'm sick of keeping it in neutral while you decide how this is going to go."

I gasp. "Me? I've told you this can't happen. I've done everything I can to make it clear that there is no *us*. I don't know what you're waiting for, Weston, but don't put it on me."

His body solidifies as I speak, his hands clutching the bench at my sides tighter until his knuckles turn white. "Is that why your body is quivering right now? Because there is no you and me? Is that why every time I see you, you lick those full lips and bite down on the corner as you try to look away before I notice?"

The vein in his neck pulses as he grinds his teeth together then continues, "Is that why I can smell how turned on you are right now? You want me, Tor. I know you do. The only person you're fooling here is yourself. I can't do this shit anymore."

With that, he pushes away from me with a shove and storms out of the room. The back door slams shut a moment later, and I let out the shuddering cry I managed to hold in while he spoke.

I slump forward, resting my head on my folded arms, and cry in earnest.

How did I let this happen?

Chapter Fourteen

Victoria

Five Months Ago . . .

"Alright, woman. Spill."

I turn around to find Vera in the very place her son had stood just a few weeks earlier. "Hey, V, what's up?" I mumble over my shoulder and keep working.

The grating sound of her dragging a stool across the room irritates on my already fragile nerves. When she plonks down beside me, I eye her cautiously. We haven't had our weekly wine-and-dine in I can't remember how long.

I'd started pulling away from Vera when it became clear to me that I'd developed feelings for her son. A wave of nausea rolls through me, and I close my eyes as I breathe through it.

"*What's up?* That's all you have to say to me after I had to break into your house to see you? *What's up?* That's all you've got?" She glares at the side of my face, I sigh and begin packing up my tools.

She waits patiently as I set each pair of pliers in its correct spot and return all the different beads to their containers. When I am done, I turn my chair to face her. "You're right. I've been a shitty friend the last few months, and I'm sorry. I've had a lot going on and—"

"So why haven't you come to me to talk it out? Isn't that what we do? We talk our shit out? I bounce my shitty day off you, you bounce your shitty day off me, and then we drink wine and eventually laugh about it then move on."

My shoulders slump, that's how it used to be. Vera is my closest friend, and I've betrayed our friendship by falling for her son. I feel every bit as awful as I clearly am.

A tear slides down my cheek. "I can't talk to you about this stuff, V. That's the problem."

She doesn't say anything for a minute, but I can feel her eyes on me. "Okay," she finally says.

Glancing up at her, I can tell she is thinking, and I honestly don't want to know what. Vera isn't an idiot, and she knows her son well. Hell, she knows me better than nearly anybody. I have a feeling she knows what is going on but was waiting for me to approach the topic.

Unfortunately for her, that just isn't going to happen.

After another moment of awkward silence, she rolls her shoulders back and says, "What about this new business of yours? You can't talk to me about that? I actually bought one of your pieces without knowing it was yours."

"You did?" I ask, shocked. Vera isn't the type to wear beaded jewelry. Ever since we met, she's worn the same gold chain necklace, and she regularly rotates her gold rings to make room for the new ones she acquires.

She nods. "I did." Then she blushes. "I actually bought it for you." She rolls her eyes and laughs. "Imagine my surprise when I showed Weston, and he told me that was your logo on the tag."

I feel a twinge of guilt at not having shared my new passion with her, but I feel even worse at the mention of Weston. I sigh deeply. "Sorry, again. Shitty friend of the year award goes to me," I joke.

But Vera doesn't laugh. "Not yet it doesn't, but if you break my son's heart, it will."

Then, she stands and heads to the door. She pauses in the frame and looks back over her shoulder, catching my stunned expression, but choosing to ignore it. "I'll be here for the wining and dining you owe me tomorrow night at six." She winks then continues on her way.

I sit there, blinking at the empty doorway, wondering if I just imagined that conversation.

But true to her word, Vera arrives the next evening at six, letting herself in the back sliding door with two bottles of wine in hand. "Alright, let's get the awkward shit out of the way first so we can enjoy this wine?" she announces cheerfully as she plonks the bottles down on the kitchen island between us.

I frown as I try to find the words to apologize.

"Don't go looking like that, Tory. I'm not here to bust your buns, honey. But I need to lay it out so we can move forward. Okay?" She says, smiling wide.

Why is she smiling like that? It is a smile I've never seen her wear before, and I hope I never do again. It's a cross between the crazed smile of The Joker and the creepy one of the Cheshire Cat. "Uh, V... I, umm..." I stumble for the right words.

She throws her head back and laughs at my obvious discomfort.

"This isn't funny, V. And I think I'm going to need something stronger than wine for this conversation," I mutter, turning around to rummage through the cupboards, looking for anything with a high alcohol content.

I find a bottle of gin, grab it and two shot glasses, then turn back to my clearly insane friend. "I don't know if I should share this with you. I'm getting the vibe you already helped yourself before you came over."

Vera raises one perfectly sculpted brow and crosses her arms. "If you saw the look on your face when I walked in here, you'd be laughing too."

"If I thought my friend was screwing my son, I wouldn't be laughing." The words tumble out before I realize what I am saying.

Vera goes still. "So things have changed between last night and now?" she asks.

I frown again. "No." I draw the word out, wondering what is going on.

She huffs, grabs a stool, drags it around to my side of the counter, and commands, "Sit," before returning to her own side and sitting down. She steeples her fingers as she waits for me to comply.

Sitting down, I watch her grab the bottle of gin and fill both glasses to the brim then carefully she slides them both to me. "I have a feeling you're going to need this more than I will. I've had time to come to my conclusions. I've had time to process all the facts. You haven't. So drink up."

Not wanting to see what she'll do if I didn't listen, I pick up the first shot and down it. When that doesn't stop my nerves from trying to escape my body, I chase it with the second.

"Okay, here it is. Weston talks to me, you know that. I've known how he's felt about you since he was seventeen."

My eyes widen, and I swallow back the gin as it tries to make a reappearance.

"That boy's been crazy about you for years. You know it, so don't even try denying it. You also know it isn't a schoolboy crush. He wouldn't still be holding on to this if it was. He's twenty-two, Tory, he's a grown man now."

Now that the gin has settled back in my stomach, I reach for the bottle and skip the glass, putting it straight to my lips and taking a long swig.

Vera rolls her eyes. "You're being dramatic," she says, prying the bottle from my hands.

"Hey, I wasn't done with that," I snap.

She rolls her eyes again. "I want you to remember this conversation, not pass out before I've said what I need to say."

I stick out my tongue. "When did you get so bossy?"

"When my son came home looking like he'd just lost hope. I've been telling him for years that he just needs to wait, that when the time is right, everything will fall into place. That hope kept him going, kept him motivated, but now it's gone."

Blinking back tears, I process Vera's words. She told him it would work out? Why? "Did you think he would grow out of it?" I ask.

"Haven't you been listening? This isn't a crush, Victoria. Weston is in love with you, and that isn't going to change anytime soon. So, what are you going to do about it?"

I jerk back, nearly toppling off my stool. I press my hand to my chest. "Me? I'm not doing anything. I keep saying no. I swear, V."

She looks up to the ceiling and mutters something like, "*Give me strength,*" then glares at me. "I know you have, honey. But you don't want to. You're making it more complicated than it needs to be."

Slumping forward, I press my forehead to the cool countertop. "I don't know what you want me to do? Are you telling me to stay away or to go to him? Because it sounds like you're telling me I should be with him, but that can't be right. He could be my *son*."

Vera takes a deep breath. "When did you get so stupid? He could *not* be your son. Ten-year-olds don't give birth, Tory. If you were Luke's mom, sure, I'd be kicking your ass right now, but you're not. You became Finn's mother by default. This is different, and you damn well know that. That's why I'm okay with it."

My confusion has risen to unprecedented levels. Never in a million years did I think Vera would be okay with Weston and me being together. But here she is, practically shoving me towards him.

Sitting up, I eye her thoughtfully. "This isn't normal motherly behavior," I say, feeling like I need to put it out there.

Vera shrugs. "We're not normal mothers, you and I."

"Touché," I mutter. "So, just to be clear, you want me to do sexually perverted things to your son?"

She shudders. "If that's what you two are into. I'd just like to state right now, before you get ahead of yourself, this is one relationship I won't be requiring details about. As in, ever. I'm okay with you two doing the dirty, but I don't want to know about it. Am I clear?"

I laugh. "You're so weird."

"I know. I accepted that a long time ago. Acceptance is the key to moving forward," she muses.

"Getting philosophical now, are we?" I tease.

And just like that, the awkwardness is gone. Vera and I are back to normal.

I have no idea what to do with what she's told me, but it's taken a weight off my shoulders, being able to talk to her again.

Chapter Fifteen

Victoria

Three Months Ago . . .

Wedding plans are taking up a huge chunk of my time. Usually, it's the mother of the bride who plays a big role in this sort of thing, but Nixie has insisted her mother isn't interested, and she wants my help. So, here I am, eating my eighth sample of wedding cake just to make sure it's the right choice.

"You're going to make yourself sick," Weston murmurs from the seat across from me.

We've been getting along better in the last two months, and I can't help but think I have Vera to thank for it. Weston's stopped pushing me, and we've found the friendship we used to enjoy again.

I grin at him. "It'll be totally worth it. Have you tried this one?"

He raises a brow. "Yep, that's the one they decided on an hour ago, yeah?"

Nodding, I shovel another piece into my mouth. "Uh-ha, I'm just doing quality control. You know, making sure each batch is consistently awesome."

Weston shakes his head then reaches over with his fork and stabs a piece of *my* cake. He pauses before licking his lips then slowly opening his mouth and placing the cake inside. He closes his eyes as he chews slowly then swallows. A soft moan of approval vibrates up his throat as I watch his Adam's apple bob up and down.

I'm completely fixated, unable to look away. The asshole is messing with me. But I can't stop myself from watching his every move. When he opens his eyes and catches mine, he smiles like the cat who got the cream. I narrow my eyes on him. "Tease," I mutter.

His smile widens. "The offer's always been open to you, Tor. You're the one teasing me."

My eyes widen. "I am not."

He tilts his head to the side and raises a brow. "Oh, really? What would you call it then? I've been sitting here with a boner, watching you eat cake for the last two hours."

I scoff. "That's what happens when you take Viagra instead of your multivitamin in the morning."

Laughter bursts from his lips. "Viagra? You and I both know I've never needed help getting it up when you're in the room." The mirth has disappeared from his eyes; now they shine with lust and dirty thoughts.

Swallowing hard, I have to look away, otherwise I fear I'll launch myself across the table and ravage him to within an inch of his life. And there are several reasons I can't do that. One being my son sitting at the other end of the table, currently glaring at his best friend.

"Please tell me you are not putting the moves on my mom again?" Finn groans.

Weston turns his attention to Finn and grins. "I've never stopped, bro." Then he winks.

"Well, maybe you should—at least when I'm in the same room. It's getting harder and harder not to beat your ass every time you do it," Finn grumbles.

Weston simply shrugs in reply. "I'll see what I can do."

"Thanks." Sarcasm drips from Finn's tone.

I choose that moment to speak up. "Okay, so now that I've sufficiently gorged myself on cake, can you place your order? Otherwise, I'm going to keep eating, and then you'll be rolling me out of here."

Nixie laughs, but the tension between Finn and Weston is still in the air. Nix notices and grabs onto Finn's arm and whispers something in his ear. Whatever she says turns his attention back to her, and judging by the lustful way he is staring at her, I figure whatever she said was kinky.

That's when Luke speaks up. I'd completely forgotten he and Beth were even here with us. I was so focused on the cake, then Weston, that I'd blocked everything else out. "Dude, he's going to snap one day and break your pretty face."

Weston laughs. "Yeah, nah, that's not going to happen. He loves my pretty face."

Luke doesn't look convinced. "Yeah, but, dude"—his eyes flick to me then back to Weston—"she's his mom. It's a clear violation of the Bro Code."

I choose to remain silent, nothing I can say will help this conversation. But Weston doesn't agree.

His eyes narrow on Luke. "You do realize she's not his

biological mother, right? So, technically, Bro Code doesn't apply here."

Luke frowns. "She's not?"

Seriously? Do I look old enough to be Finn's birth mother? God, I hope not. I clear my throat. "No, I'm not Finn's biological mother, but he's still my son—has been since he was ten years old. His mother was my sister."

This isn't something we speak about much. And I haven't really thought too much about it. I've spoken to Vera about it, and obviously Weston knows. But I haven't thought about what others think about Finn's and my relationship.

Luke slowly nods. "Makes sense. You're too hot to be that old."

A serious blush creeps up my neck. "Uh, thank you. I think."

Weston's fist shoots out and punches Luke in the shoulder. "Eyes off. I called dibs."

Luke rubs his shoulder. "I figured," he mutters.

"Uh, sorry to burst your bubble, but nobody has dibs on me," I say before they can continue.

Luke's eyes light up. "So, you're available."

Weston's fist once again shoots out, but this time, he puts more force behind the hit. "No, she's not."

I cross my arms across my chest. "Since when?" I demand.

All of a sudden, all eyes are on me. I swallow. I hadn't meant to speak so loudly.

"What's going on?" Finn asks, having been brought out of his and Nixie's impromptu make-out session.

My eyes shoot to him. "Nothin'. I've gotta go. All this cake is calling my name, and I'm losing the strength to resist. If I stay any longer, I won't fit in my dress for the wedding." I stand up and kiss Nixie's cheek then scruff up Finn's hair and kiss his cheek too. "Bye, guys." Then, I scurry out of there.

Once in my car, I fly out of the parking lot and away from a conversation I'm still not ready for.

I MANAGE TO AVOID WESTON THE FOLLOWING WEEK, BUT COME Saturday, there is a knock on the doorframe to my workshop. I turn my head to see him leaning against the frame. "Hey," I mumble as I turn my focus back to the piece I am assembling.

"You been avoiding me again, Tor?" he asks.

I don't turn back, but I reply honestly, "A little."

"Because of last weekend?" he questions.

"Yep. I'm not ready to continue that conversation, so if that's why you're here, you can leave." I fiddle with the piece of wire that isn't doing what it is supposed to.

He drags a chair over to sit by me as I work. I glance at him from the corner of my eye; he is watching my hands as I work. "You're really good at this," he murmurs.

"Thanks." I don't know what else to say, and it doesn't seem like he's going to push the relationship bounds again today, so I relax and keep working.

We sit in comfortable silence for a few more minutes, and it is actually really nice. It doesn't feel weird having him in my space like I thought it would.

"I just need to ask you one thing, then I'll drop it," Weston says quietly.

I put my tools down and turn to face him. "Okay."

He nods and licks his lips. My gaze fixates on his tongue until it slips back inside his mouth, then I regain my focus, clear my throat and say, "Shoot."

"Am I wasting my time here? Will you ever be ready?" His eyes never leave mine as he speaks.

I blink a few times before I find my voice. "That is two questions." I laugh drily, trying to lighten the moment, but nothing but my answer can do that. I close my eyes, take a deep breath, and clear my mind of everything but the two of us.

When I open them, I tell him the truth. "You're right, I do want to be with you. It's just not that simple."

He opens his mouth to speak, but I hold up my hand, stopping him. "Let me get this all out first." I wait for him to nod, then continue. "Finn isn't going to be happy about it. And he's my priority. I have to talk to him before I even think about entering into anything with you."

I don't realize I'm reaching for him until my palm comes into contact with his stubbled cheek. He closes his eyes, leaning into my touch, and my thumb grazes lightly over his bottom lip. "I don't know when it will be the right time to talk to him, and I don't expect you to sit around waiting for it."

Sighing, I close my eyes. "You've been so patient with me, and I've rejected you at every turn. I can't ask you for more time, you've already given me so much."

The next thing I know, Weston's picking me up and bringing me onto his lap. His large hands grip my thighs as he presses his forehead to mine. "I have so much more to give. And I will. When you're ready."

A sob wrenches from deep within my chest as all my emotions flood to the surface. "I can't push you away again, but I can't lie to him."

Weston's hands move from my thighs, up my back, bringing me closer. "Then I won't ask you again until you've spoken to him."

Relief, pure and sweet, fills my lungs, and I cry harder. Weston strokes my back with his fingertips. "Shhh, we're on the same page now. Everything will be okay."

I slump against his shoulder. "I know," I whisper.

After carrying guilt, fear, and shame around for so long, when it is lifted, all I can do is cry with relief as I breathe in Weston's scent, filling my heart with hope for the first time in a long time.

I'm not sure how long we sit like that, me straddling his lap, snuggling into his shoulder while he gently strokes my back. But when my tears have dried, I know it is time to move. Pressing my hands to his firm shoulders, I push myself into a sitting position then grin at him.

I've never seen him so happy. He's practically glowing.

His hand slides up the back of my neck, tangling in my hair as he brings my face closer to his. "Just one to hold me over," he murmurs before his lips caress mine and he steals my breath.

Nothing has ever felt so right.

My hands move from his shoulders into his hair as his tongue slides across the seam of my lips. I whimper and open for him just as his fist clenches the hair at my nape. "I can't wait to have all of you," he groans against my lips, and I smile, knowing it won't be long before I give myself to him.

Now that I have let go of everything that's been holding

me back and admitted my feelings for him, all I have to do is talk to Finn.

Weston brushes one more kiss against my lips. "I won't push you to talk to him, but please, don't wait too long."

I nod and slide off his lap onto wobbly legs. "I won't."

Chapter Sixteen

Victoria

Two Months Ago . . .

Finding the right time to talk to your son about wanting to start a relationship with his best friend is apparently impossible. Every time I think I can broach the topic, the words I've practiced flee from my mind, and I end up babbling about random things like peanut butter M&M's versus crispy ones—or something equally unimportant.

Today, we had yet another one of these strangely random conversations.

I've just gotten home when my cell chimes with a text. I glance at the screen and smile at Weston's name staring back at me.

I trudge down the hallway into my room, flop onto my bed, then open the text.

WESTON: You look particularly miserable today.

I frown. *When did he see me?* I tap out a reply.

TORY: How would you know?

The little dots appear immediately.

WESTON: Saw you get home just now. What's up?

Sighing deeply, I decide I should tell him what is going on. He's remained true to his word and backed off on the relationship front. I see him around, and things between us are almost normal, except for the cheeky texts I get when we are in a group setting and Luke pretends to flirt with me.

I chew on my lip, trying to find the right thing to tell him.

TORY: I tried to talk to Finn today. It didn't go to plan. It never does. I start babbling about random crap like swans being the only birds with an external penis.

The dots take a little longer to appear this time.

WESTON: Do you want me to talk to him?

As much as I would love to not have this conversation with Finn, it has to be me.

TORY: Thanks, but no. It needs to come from me.

This time, the dots don't come up at all. But a tap on my semi-closed bedroom door does. I lift my head in time to see Weston strolling in like he owns the place. I arch a brow. "What are you doing here?"

He shrugs. "Believe it or not, I'm not big on texting. Especially when the person I'm texting is right next door."

My head flops back against the pillow. "Fair enough."

"So, do I even want to know how you know about swan dicks?"

I shake my head. "Probably not."

The bed dips as he sits on the edge then shuffles until he's leaning against the headboard. He relaxes, crossing his arms behind his head, and I notice a new tattoo—at least, I think it's new.

Reaching up, I glide my finger over it. It's still slightly raised, confirming it's newness. "When'd you get this?" I ask as my fingertip traces the intricate arrow on the inside of his bicep.

He glances over to the spot I am touching. "Week before last. You like it?"

I nod. "Yeah. It's nice. I was going to get something similar." I reach over and grab my cell so I can pull up Pinterest and show him the design I'd chosen. When I find it, I hand my phone to him.

"Huh, it is pretty similar. You still going to get it?" he asks as he hands my phone back.

Shrugging, I take it and start looking through the other designs I'd pinned. "I think so. One day. I like the meaning behind it."

Weston smiles down at me. "Me too. That's why I got it."

I return his smile and nod. "To moving forward," I murmur as I keep scrolling through my boards.

"To moving forward," Weston seconds softly and reaches down to twirl a strand of my hair around his fingers.

We stay like that for the next hour, him playing with my

hair, me showing him designs I like, until his cell rings in his pocket.

He keeps playing with my hair as he tugs it out and answers with his free hand. "Hello," he says with a frown. "Yeah, speaking," he says after a second. Then, his hand stills, and tension rolls through him until his whole body is stiff. He sits up straight and turns, swinging his legs over the edge of the bed. He remains silent, but the phone is still pressed to his ear.

I sit up behind him and crawl closer, then his phone slides from his grasp and hits the floor. "Weston, what's wrong?" I ask as I slide up beside him.

All the color drains from his face as a sheen of sweat breaks out across his forehead. I reach for him, but he jolts before I can make contact, lurching to his feet he bursts into my bathroom, dropping to his knees and throwing up in the toilet.

Glancing down, I notice the call is still connected, and it is from an unknown number. I pick it up and hold it to my ear. "Hello?" I say softly, not knowing if I am doing the right thing or not.

"Hello, is Weston Banks still there?" the female voice on the other end asks.

I shake my head. "No, he's sick. Who is this?"

"My name is Bernice. I work with Vera, Weston's mom. Something happened at work, the ambulance came and—" She pauses, and sucks in an anguished breath.

My pulse kicks up. "What's wrong with Vera? Where is she?" I demand.

"She's gone," Bernice whispers.

"Okay, what hospital was she taken to? Where is she?" Something is very wrong; I can feel it in my bones.

A stuttered cry echoes through the line. "She's gone. She was gone before the E.M.T.'s even arrived."

I shake my head. "I don't understand. You're not making any sense." I can't let myself believe what she's implying. It isn't true. It can't be.

"They took her to St. Paul's. I'm sorry. I'm so, so, sorry." Then, the line goes silent.

My entire body is numb. I don't even feel it when my legs give out and I hit the floor with a thud. I curl into a ball and stay there. If I stay here long enough, someone will come and tell me that this is all a sick and twisted joke.

But nobody comes.

I don't know how long it takes me to pull myself together enough to check on Weston. I find him slumped against the side of the bathtub. His skin is ashen, and grief drips from his pores. I drop to my knees in front of him.

His empty gaze meets mine. "She was all I had."

My heart breaks for him.

Then it breaks for me.

Weston's mom, my best friend, Vera, is gone.

Grief overwhelms me, and I drop my head to Weston's raised knees and sob.

Somehow, I find the strength to push my pain aside, and make myself to focus on what needs to be done. My throat is tight, making it hard to speak, but I close my eyes and take a deep breath, then force words passed my lips.

"We need to go to the hospital," I tell Weston.

His gorgeous face is void of expression as he nods. He takes my hands in his before pushing to his feet, dragging me up with him.

I keep my fingers laced with his as I lead him out to my

car, then I take his hand again when I get in behind the wheel and drive us to St. Paul's.

We're ushered to a semi-private cubical, with a gurney positioned in the center of the space. Vera's body lay beneath a white sheet, and the nurse leaves us without a word.

Weston and I both stare at the gurney, neither able to move.

"Do—do you want to see her?" I eventually ask.

He blinks, his gaze unfocused as he nods once. I close the small distance and take the corner of the sheet between trembling fingers then tug it away from her face. A gut-wrenching sob tears from my throat and my knees buckle.

Weston's arms circle my waist, catching me before I hit the ground then he tugs me into his chest. His face is still blank, his eyes vacant but his hand runs up and down my spine in long soothing strokes. *How can he possibly be comforting* me *in this moment?* I lock my jaw and squeeze my eyes closed as I wind my arms around him and hold tight.

Someone clears their throat behind Weston, and I pry myself from his embrace long enough to acknowledge the man standing just inside the curtain. His words are a blur, and I'm not sure how much of what he says reaches Weston, so I listen intently in case I need to repeat it all back to him later.

The doctor explains that Vera had a brain aneurysm. She died instantly. He tells us that forty percent of ruptured brain aneurysms are fatal. And in his opinion, she was lucky, as the remaining sixty percent either die on the way to the hospital or suffer permanent debilitating brain damage.

The urge to punch him in the face for making Vera sound like she's just another statistic, is overwhelming. But

Weston's arms tighten around me as I unconsciously move towards the man.

By the time it's all over, and we return to my car, it is dark outside. I'm operating on autopilot as I drive us home, and Weston hasn't spoken a word for hours.

I pull into my driveway, then walk beside him to his front door. When he doesn't make a move to open it, I offer, "Do you want me to...?"

He shakes his head and his gaze locks with mine. His pain is raw and crippling. I take his hand and lead him back across the lawn to my house. I open the door and pull him in behind me.

His hand is cold and stiff, but he holds mine as if it is his lifeline. I give it a squeeze and tug him farther down the hall to my bedroom. He doesn't protest when I guide him to the bed and press my palm to his chest, urging him to sit.

I climb onto the bed beside him and gently nudge his shoulder to get him to lie down. Then, I curl into his side and stay there until the sun comes up the next morning.

Neither of us sleep a wink. But we don't fill the silence, our bodies giving the comfort that our words cannot. Weston holds me as tightly as I hold him. No words need to be spoken between us.

THE MORNING OF THE FUNERAL COMES, AND I HAVE NO IDEA how I've gotten here. I don't remember helping Weston make the arrangements, although I know I did. From the moment I pulled myself off my bedroom floor, until now, I've been in a daze.

Weston has spent every night at my place, in my bed.

And each night, we hold each other in silence. Those have been my only truly lucid moments in the days that have passed.

I don't try to push him to enter his own house. I know what he's feeling—the same apprehension as I'd felt when I had to walk inside of Jacq's house for the first time after she died. It was one of the hardest things I ever had to do.

It helped me heal. I'm not sure how, but it brought a closeness to her that I desperately needed in those days. I want to tell Weston that it will get better, that he will be able to breathe again without feeling the pressing weight of grief crushing his heart with every inhale.

But today is not the day. Today, another step has to be taken, and this one may well be the hardest of all.

Today, we put Vera to rest.

Today signifies the end of a beautiful life and the beginning of learning how to live without it.

Chapter Seventeen

Victoria

Six Weeks Ago . . .

Weston still hasn't gone inside his and Vera's house. A week has come and gone since the funeral, nearly two weeks since Vera passed, and I know I'm the only person who can get him to take that step.

He's stayed at my house since that first night, and even though we hold each other, there is no sexual intimacy shared between us. Just comfort.

In fact, we've barely spoken. I've tried to engage him in conversation, but he is too lost in his own thoughts to even realize that the outside world keeps on moving around him.

Everyone grieves differently—I know that—but he's worrying me.

My cell chimes with a text from Finn.

FINN: How is he today?

Finn knows Weston has been staying with me, but he doesn't know he's been sharing my bed. And now isn't not the time to have that particular conversation.

TORY: He's in the shower. Going to make him coffee and see if I can get him to go over to the house today.

The little dots pop up immediately.

FINN: Want me to come over? Help?

I think about it briefly but decide against it. I don't know how Weston will react to going into Vera's personal space—if he agrees to go, that is.

TORY: Let me try first. I'll call if I need you.

Just as I slide my phone back onto the countertop, Weston strolls into the kitchen. I turn to smile at him, but my smile fades when I see the bags under his eyes. "Have you been sleeping at all?" I ask.

He grimaces. "Maybe an hour or two here and there?"

I nod then return to fixing a couple of extra-strong coffees. The high-pitched squeak of a bar stool being pulled out grates against my ears. When I turn to him, his elbows rest on the counter as he cradles his head in his palms.

"Coffee?" I ask as I slide his mug over to him and take the stool beside his.

"Thanks," he mumbles but makes no move to take it.

Instead of asking if he wants breakfast, since I already know he'll refuse, I pick up my coffee and sip the steamy caffeinated goodness like it is my first and last coffee ever. I nudge his elbow. "Try it. I used the new hazelnut beans I got yesterday. It's really good."

He nods and picks up his mug and inhales the rich hazelnut and coffee aroma. "Smells good. Thanks." He drinks a little then puts it back down and proceeds to stare out the kitchen window across from us.

"Weston," I hedge, waiting for some kind of acknowledgment.

"Hmm," he mumbles but doesn't look at me.

"Weston, it's time. We need to go over there today. We need to start sorting out her things." I pause when his entire body stiffens. Reaching out, I place my hand over his. "I'll be there with you the whole time. I promise."

His Adam's apple bobs as he swallows. "I"—he clears his throat—"I don't know, Tor. I don't"—he heaves a heavy sigh—"I don't think I can."

I get off my stool and stand behind him, wrapping my arms around his broad body and resting my head between his shoulder blades. "You can. I'll be there beside you, every step of the way."

Tremors of suppressed emotion roll through his body, and I hold him still, absorbing all the pain and hurt that radiates through him. I would take it all away if I could, but since I can't, I will do the next best thing—help him heal.

WE STAND ON THE FRONT PORCH OF VERA'S HOUSE, SIDE BY side. Weston makes no move to open the door, so I slip my hand into his pocket, remove the keys, and open the door myself.

The air inside has grown stale and stagnant from being locked up for the past two weeks.

I take the first step inside then turn back to Weston. I twine my fingers through his, then tug him gently toward me. He grimaces as he comes to me then wraps his arms around me so tight I can barely breathe.

He squeezes a little tighter then loosens his grip. “Thank you. For everything,” he murmurs into my ear. “I couldn’t have done any of this without you.” His voice is thick with emotion as he speaks.

“I would do anything to make this easier for you. *Anything*.”

Weston lifts his head, our gazes locking. His flicks between my eyes and lips. “Kiss me, Tory.” His voice trembles with pent-up need.

My body sparks to life right there in the entryway of Vera’s house. I don’t respond with my words. Instead, I use my body. I slide my hands along his shoulders, up his neck, and into his hair, drawing his face down to mine as I reach up on my tiptoes and press my lips to his.

This kiss isn’t urgent. We don’t hurry. There is no rush.

I savor the taste of him on my lips, the smell of him engulfing me. My fingers splay out then fist in his hair, urging him to take what he needs from me.

And he does.

His hands go to my hips and lift me off the ground. He turns us, kicking the door closed with his foot then pinning me against it with his firm body.

“Weston,” I murmur against his lush lips.

He pulls back briefly to gaze at me. “Tor,” he whispers as his fingertips trail down my cheek to skate across my lips.

The torment and sorrow is still there in his deep eyes, but it has been pushed to the back, making way for lust and need.

The hand that is still on my waist squeezes as he brings his mouth back to mine, making me moan and arch my back, pushing myself further into him.

Minutes or hours later—I'm not sure—Weston breaks away from my lips and rests his head on my shoulder. I loosen my grip on his hair and begin to stroke my fingers against his scalp.

He releases a deep, contented sigh.

"Come on, let's get started," I say softly against the top of his head.

This time, there is no resistance. He nods slowly and stands to his full height. "I'm ready."

Chapter Eighteen

Victoria

Four Weeks Ago . . .

We all banded together to clear out Vera's things, and the house is now up for sale. I'd questioned Weston about his choice to sell the house so soon, but he was adamant that was what he wanted to do. He'd said it was too hard to stay there without her. And I knew what he meant.

I'd found it hard to stay in Jacq's house, but I'd done it for Finn.

Weston continues to stay at my place, and we still haven't crossed any relationship lines. In fact, we haven't kissed since the day we went to the house for the first time, two weeks ago.

The right time to talk to Finn is becoming harder and harder to find. With wedding plans taking up a big chunk of my time and my jewelry business growing, I am struggling to catch my breath.

But Weston never pushes about it. He doesn't even bring

it up. And while that makes it easier on me, I am beginning to grow desperate to cross that line with him. I want to hold his hand in public. I want to kiss him when he gets home from work. I want to wash his back as he showers.

If I was being completely honest with myself, I'd just admit I want to get down and dirty with him. It is pure torture, sleeping in his arms every night without touching him the way I ache to. Without caving to my constant fantasies—and there are a lot of fantasies these days.

I have never, in all my life, been this sexually frustrated.

And I can't do any of those things until I speak to Finn. A perfect time isn't going to just present itself, I have to *make* the time.

That's when I begin plotting, devising my plan of attack.

Little did I know, Weston was also plotting and coming up with his own plan to get our future as a couple on track.

Two Weeks Ago . . .

With the wedding just weeks away, my head is constantly spinning. With dress fittings, collecting RSVPs, confirming with caterers, finding the perfect pair of shoes, getting through make-up and hairstyle trials, and a million other little things that need to be handled, I've nearly forgotten my own name.

It is at this point that I'm glad Finn is an only child. I'm not sure if I could go through all of this again.

Weddings are the definition of stressful.

But this one will be perfect, even if I have to nearly kill myself making sure of it.

And unfortunately, that means waiting to broach the topic of Weston and I as a couple until after it is all over.

My body cringes at the knowledge that I will be waiting, at the very least, another two weeks to touch Weston—which is actually four weeks in reality, since Finn and Nix are off on their honeymoon the night of the wedding for two weeks of newly wedded bliss.

My high-strung libido screams at me to throw my plan in the dumpster and go talk to Finn right now so I can get my hot little hands all over Weston's incredible body.

But my brain refuses to make these last few weeks till the wedding any more stressful on Finn than they already are.

One Week Ago . . .

I'm sound asleep, having another one of my fantastic dreams involving Weston hovering above me, raining soft kisses and barely there licks down my throat, across my collarbone, and—

Wait.

My eyes shoot open to find my fantasy has come to life.

Weston *is* hovering over me in bed, fire blazing in his eyes as they meet mine briefly before returning his attention to my chest. My back arches as a needy moan is wrenched from my throat.

He presses his hips into me, and I feel every inch of him. My body shudders with appreciation.

Then, my brain wakes up and ruins everything.

"Wait, we have to stop," I whine.

"You don't sound very convincing, Tory," he mumbles

right before sucking my left nipple into the warmth of his mouth.

My back arches higher, and my hands fly into his hair, holding him there. And again, my brain speaks up. I swallow hard. "Weston, we can't. Not yet."

Ever so slowly he pulls back. "I know. Was just giving you a little preview of things to come." He winks at me then climbs off the bed and heads to my adjoining bathroom.

I watch him go in all his naked glory. I have to be insane to let that body out of my bed without taking full advantage of the situation.

That or I am a good mom? That's what I tell myself as I slide out of bed and go to make myself a strong coffee and hope that it'll be enough to keep me away from the temptation currently washing up in my shower.

The next morning, Weston wakes me in a similar way.

This time, he's running his talented tongue down my spine after sucking gently on my neck, coming to rest against my ass. Then he bites it, climbs out of bed, and heads for the shower.

I want to cry. My body aches for a release. I tremble with need and desperation. He's doing this on purpose. I guess he's had enough of waiting for me to talk to Finn.

Again, the following morning, I'm privy to another one of Weston's many talents. And I can't do a thing about it but lie there and enjoy it for mere moments before he pulls away and strides to shower.

I've become a walking nightmare, wound so tight I snap at the slightest thing.

"Jesus, Tory, I've never seen you go off on someone like that before," Luke says after I'd blown a gasket on the phone to the caterer.

Dropping my head into my hands, I sigh. He's right. I'm taking my sexual frustration out on innocent bystanders. But I can't help it.

Weston grins from across the table. "Anyone would think you need to get laid. You seem super tense," he teases with a proud smirk.

My jaw drops. Oh, hell no! "This is all your fault!" I accuse.

He feigns innocence. "My fault? What'd I do?"

Luke's ears perk up as he glances between the two of us, Weston grinning like a fool and me glaring like I want his balls to fall off. And in all honesty, at that very moment, that's exactly what I want.

I stand, lean toward him, and slam my hands against the solid timber table. "You're a pain in my ass, Weston Banks."

His grin widens further. "Glad to be of service," he says with a wink.

Steam is pouring from my ears; I am sure of it. I glance around the surrounding surface, looking for something, anything to inflict pain on him. Right as my eyes land on a three-quarter full bottle of Coke, Luke's hand shoots out and snatches it up before I can.

"That's mine. Here." He hands me a bamboo stirring spoon. "Use this. It'll sting more."

I jerk it from his hand and go for Weston's bicep, but he springs out of his chair and takes off out the front door. "That is a clear violation of Bro Code, Luke!" he yells as he runs away like a little girl.

I mumble obscenities under my breath as I sit back down.

"For real, though, Tory, are you okay? I'm not saying that

Wes is right, because I'd never live it down, but you do look like you need to get some," Luke says.

A frown wrinkles my forehead, then I have an idea. I turn my frown upside down, a seductive smile curving my lips. I bat my lashes at Luke and tilt my head to the side. "Are you offering, Luke?"

Luke's eyes bulge. "Are you for real?"

I shrug. "Maybe. It has been a while."

Before Luke can answer, Weston marches back inside. "Oh, fuck no. Don't even think about it!" he seethes at Luke then turns his glare on me. "You're not funny."

Now, I am the one grinning. "Whatever do you mean?"

He clenches his teeth, leans forward, and places his balled fists on the table between us, Luke completely forgotten. "You *know* what I mean, Tory. You. Are. Mine."

The possession in his tone makes me shiver. Placing my hands on the table between us, I slowly stand, coming face to face with him. So close his breath ghosts over my mouth. My tongue flicks out to wet my suddenly dry lips. "Not yet, I'm not. But soon," I whisper, then before I lose myself and kiss him, I spin on my heel and take off to my bedroom, locking the door behind me.

Chapter Nineteen

Victoria

Present Day. . . The Wedding. . .

Weston hasn't relented with his morning assaults until today, and that isn't by choice. Finn, Weston, and Luke all stayed at Finn's place last night, and Nixie and Beth stayed at mine.

While it is a relief not having him amp me up even more, I did miss his presence in my bed through the night. I've grown used to him holding me, and I found myself tossing and turning half the night, trying to get comfortable without him.

My eyes flick open as the alarm blasts out Bruno Mars' "Marry You" at top volume. I smile. Today, after months of stress and grief, we will celebrate.

My heart clenches at the thought of Jacq and Vera missing this day. I miss them both fiercely. But I know, deep down, they will always be with all of us. And just like she has at other times when I've needed her most, I swear I can feel

Jacq here with me, telling me how proud she is of me and the life Finn and I have built without her.

A single tear slides down my cheek, but it's in happiness.

By the time I drag myself out of bed and into the shower, I can already hear Beth and Nixie rummaging around the kitchen, making coffee, I presume.

I shower quickly—well, as quickly as I can, considering I need to shave everything, even though I'd had every inch waxed late last week. I just want to make sure everything is as smooth as it can be.

The dresses Nixie has chosen for Beth and I are similar to hers but not as poofy. In true Nixie fashion, our dresses are anything but traditional. And I love them.

They are strapless with plunging backs that are held together with laces. The hot-pink bodice is snug to the waist then flares out in layers of pink and cream tulle that ends at our knees.

And Nixie's, oh my God... Nixie looks amazing in her mostly cream dress. She refuses to get married in white, so her dress is the opposite of ours. Where ours have the pink bodice, hers is cream and her layered tulle skirts puff right out, like a true princess, except with a flash of the bright pink thrown in every couple of layers.

All our dresses end at the knee. Nix has matched hers with hot-pink, open-toe platform heels. And Beth and I have hot-pink-fading-into-cream in the same style.

When we're all dressed, hair and make-up ready, and the photographer has done her thing, I take Nixie aside to have a quick chat before we leave.

"Nix, you know I already love you like a daughter, but I need to thank you before this day gets away from us. You have made Finn's life complete. You gave him love when he needed it most. You, Nix"—I pause to draw a deep breath and pull myself together—"You make him happy. And I can never thank you enough for loving him like you do."

Nixie sniffles. "Thank you, but, dude, you're going to make my makeup smear. And neither of us know how to fix this crap, so stop with the emotional speeches, okay? The makeup chick already left, and if you make me cry, I'm going to look like a racoon at my own damn wedding."

We laugh and hug it out, but I have to squeeze my eyes shut to keep my tears at bay. "You'd be the sexiest racoon bride there ever was," I whisper in her ear before pulling away from her. She laughs again, and I take her hand. "You ready for this?"

Her eyes light with excitement. "Hell yeah! Let's go get me a husband!" She grins.

PULLING UP AT THE ENTRANCE TO THE BOTANICAL GARDENS, the three of us shimmy out of the car. We can see the boys in the distance, standing under a huge raintree with hanging vases filled with flowers and candles, giving the old tree an ethereal feel.

Beth and I move forward to take our positions around the corner from the make-shift aisle the boys had made using old timber pallets. Beth will walk down first and join Luke, then I—shit, I need to pull myself together—I will walk down and take my place beside Weston.

It has only been twelve hours since I saw him, but I've missed him.

Then, the music starts, and I take a deep, steadying breath and listen to "Teagan and Sara" sing I Was Married.

We've timed the walk perfectly, so when the right word comes, Beth begins to walk down the aisle.

And then it's my turn. As soon as I step around the corner, my eyes shoot first to Finn. He looks fantastic in a tailored navy-blue suit with a hot-pink tie. My eyes water up. My boy is all grown up. And what an incredible man he's grown to be. Pride swells my heart.

Then, my gaze shifts to the man beside him—Weston. He is absolutely breathtaking. His eyes appear even darker in the navy suit. And he only has eyes for me. They bore into mine, and my breath hitches. My mouth is suddenly dry, my heart lodges in my throat, and I am fully consumed by him.

When I reach his side, he takes my hand and loops it through the crook of his elbow. At his touch, a spark of electricity runs through my entire body, making me feel dizzy. Then, his fingertips graze my cheek, and I shudder.

"You look incredible, Victoria," he whispers.

My heels bring my height up closer to his mouth now, and I can feel his erratic breathing against my cheek. He's clearly as affected by me as I am by him, and my smile widens.

Before I know it, the ceremony has started and finished, and the celebrant is proclaiming Finn and Nixie as Mr. and Mrs. Finn Dixon.

Chapter Twenty

Victoria

AFTER POSING FOR A MILLION AND ONE PHOTOS, WE'RE ON OUR way to the reception. My skin is flushed from the constant feel of Weston's eyes on me. He throws his arm around my shoulder when we climb into the back of our car. "I can't not touch you," he murmurs against my throat as his lips press little kisses there.

Awareness shoots through me. I want his touch—so much—but I still haven't spoken to Finn.

For a brief moment, I close my eyes and enjoy his touch, letting my head roll to the side, giving him better access.

"Do you have any idea what you do to me?" his husky voice whispers while nibbling on my ear lobe. Then, his hand takes mine and brings it to his crotch.

My palm presses against what is, without a doubt, an impressive hard-on. I can't help it; my fingers tighten around his length, but my words contradict my actions. "I can't... we can't... not yet," I moan.

Weston has moved so he is on his knees in front of me, his hands braced on my knees, pushing them open as I lean forward so as not to lose my grip on him. Our faces are so close. I swallow hard. Everything I want in this moment is shining in his eyes as they bore into mine.

Promises of earth-shattering sex and orgasms that will send me to the stars are looking right at me, and I have to refuse.

My hand drops away from him and comes back to rest in my lap as I sit back against the seat. Weston's eyes narrow. "Is there ever going to be a right time for us?" he asks.

I sit back up and cup his jaw between my hands. "Yes, I promise." I press my forehead to his and breathe him in. "As soon as they get back from their honeymoon, I'll talk to him then."

Weston shakes his head softly. "Are you sure about that? Sure you won't come up with another excuse about why it's the wrong time? Because that's what this feels like—like I'm your dirty little secret you're too afraid to tell anyone about."

My eyes widen, and I pull back enough to meet his intense gaze. "No, you know that's not true. I want to be with you more than anything. I swear." I press a soft kiss against his lips. "But I can't lose Finn in the process. Just two more weeks, I promise you. I'll talk to him as soon as they get back."

He sighs and moves back onto the seat beside me. He takes my hand in his and holds it for the rest of the drive to the reception. But he doesn't speak again.

Guilt over how I've made him feel eats at me. If I could be sure Finn wouldn't react badly, I'd tell him tonight—right now—but I'm not sure. I have no idea how he'll react.

We arrive at the restaurant about ten minutes later, and Weston helps me out of the car like the gentleman he is.

"Thank you," I whisper, yet he only gives a slight nod in response. My shoulders sag. I hate this.

Finn, Nix, Luke, and Beth have already arrived, so we stroll over to join them in the foyer of the restaurant. I've never seen Finn so happy; it's infectious. I smile as I take in his lovestruck gaze locked in on Nixie.

They are so perfect for each other. I couldn't be happier for them. But myself? I really need to talk to Finn.

THE MEALS ARE DELICIOUS, AND THE WINE IS A-FLOWIN'—thankfully, because I have a speech to make, and I know it's going to get messy. When the MC announces that it's my turn, I down the remainder of my glass, stand on unsteady feet, then accept the microphone from his outstretched hand.

Here goes nothin'... "Hi, everyone. I'm going to keep it short and sweet, just like our beautiful bride tonight." I shoot Nixie a little wink, and she grins back as a blush fills her cheeks. "First, as Finn's mom, I'd like to thank everyone for coming and showing your support today. I know it means a lot to Finn and Nixie that you've come to share this special day with them, but it means so much to me too.

"Finn, my amazing boy, I'm so proud of you. You have grown to be a man that not only am I proud to call my son, but now Nixie is proud to call her husband. And Nix, my girl, I know you will look after him, you already do by just being you.

"So, I will leave you with this tiny piece of advice: Hold each other pure and true. You are all each other will ever need as long as you never stop saying those magical words, I love you."

I hand the microphone back to the MC then wobble back to my seat, both emotional and a teensy-tiny bit tipsy.

Weston pulls my chair out for me, and I plonk down in it gratefully. Then, he takes his place at the makeshift podium to deliver his best man speech.

He clears his throat and squeezes the mic in his hand. "Uh, well, we all know I'm not one for speeches, but it is my duty as best man and best friend to embarrass the shit out of Finn, so here goes. Nix, you should have seen the pathetic mess Finn became when you guys broke up back in high school. I'm talkin' total breakdown, emotional-little-bitch territory. He was so pathetic I considered making him hand in his man card.

"Anyway, the point is, without you, he's a whiny little bitch, so thank you, Nix, for taking his sorry ass back and kissing it all better. You've made my life a lot easier." He shoots a wink at her then hands the mic back to the MC.

On his way back past Finn, he punches him in the shoulder, and Finn takes it with pride. When he sits back down beside me, I lean into him and whisper, "Nice speech, best man."

He nods in acknowledgement but still doesn't speak to me. He's still upset with me, and I can't blame him. I feel like a colossal bitch. Signaling the waiter, I ordered a gin and tonic, with more gin than tonic. I'm going to need it to get through this night with a broody Weston at my side.

Before my drink reaches my hot little hands, it is time for the first dance. The whole bridal party comes to stand by the dance floor as Finn and Nixie gaze into each other's eyes while slowly making their way around the floor. They chose

Kissing You by Des'ree, and the music fills the room with a sultry atmosphere.

When it's time, Weston takes my hand, Luke takes Beth's and we all step onto the dancefloor. We begin to move around the room to the smooth rhythm of the song.

But even while we dance, Weston won't make eye contact with me. As the song bleeds into Sweet Baby by Macy Grey and more couples fill the floor, I grow tired of him ignoring me.

I slide my hands up his shoulders to rest around his neck as I gently run my fingers through the hair at the base of his skull. He shivers, then grits his teeth. "Weston, come on, look at me," I plead softly.

He closes his eyes tightly for a moment. When he opens them and focuses on me, they are full of regret. "I'm sorry. It's just hard having you so close and not being able to touch you the way I want to. The way I *need* to."

"I know, it's okay, I get it," I whisper.

Taking a deep breath, he shakes his head gently. "It's not. I shouldn't have taken it out on you."

I sigh and rest my cheek on his shoulder as the song moves into another. I don't want to stop dancing; I want to stay in his arms all night.

Chapter Twenty-One

Victoria

We dance together until a man I don't recognize approaches Weston from behind and taps him on the shoulder. Weston peers back at the guy and quirks a brow.

"May I cut in?" the guy asks.

Weston's gaze turns lethal and my brows furrow. I have no idea who he is. "I'm sorry, what's your name?"

He's really good-looking. He has this silver-fox thing going on. Imagine a middle-aged Harrison Ford type with slight greying by his temples. He grins at my blatant perusal of him and extends his hand to me. Once I place mine in his, he introduces himself.

"I'm Nixie's single, baggage-free uncle, Chad." His eyes glitter with mirth.

I chuckle. "Ah, nice to meet you, Chad. I assume you know who I am since you're the one trying to cut in on my best man time." I raise a brow as I wait for his reply.

Weston still has one hand curled around me, and his grip tightens at the mention of Chad's single status. I slide my palm down and rest it over his to reassure him.

Chad smirks. "I believe I'm supposed to be your designated wedding sex."

I choke on air. Weston's whole body tenses. I glance at him to find his jaw clenched tight and his free hand balled into a fist. And judging by his stance, he's holding back from kicking Chad's ass by a very thin thread. I turn into him, placing myself between the two.

"Can you give me a minute?" I ask Weston, and his eyes narrow dangerously on me. I move slightly closer and whisper, "Let me get to the bottom of this, then I'll come find you."

His response is a stiff nod, then he's gone, disappearing into the crowd. Before I even have a chance to feel guilty for sending him away, a hand lands on my hip, spinning my body back to face Chad.

He moves in with smooth, precise movements, taking my hips in his hands, not my waist. My eyes bulge. "Uh, Chad, might I ask where you got the impression that I need wedding sex arranged for me?" I ask as I move his hands up to my waist.

A single brow is his instant response. "Are you disappointed?"

I rear back slightly. "Ah, well, no. I mean, I'm not—" I huff. "Who asked you to be my wedding sex?"

His hands slowly move back down to my hips again, and I don't bother moving them again. He isn't being creepy about it; I just feel weird having another man's hands on me.

"Nixie may have mentioned that she thought you could do with a little stress relief," he murmurs as he twirls me around the dancefloor.

What the actual fuck? I blink at him. My daughter-in-law

set me up with her uncle for wedding sex? I thought this shit only happened in movies.

I clear my throat. "Well, I'm really sorry to disappoint you, Chad, but I won't be requiring your services tonight after all. But thanks for the effort, you look fantastic. I'm sure there are other single ladies waiting in the wings for an eligible bachelor such as yourself to sweep them off their feet."

He smiles and nods. "I figured as much, but I had to give it a shot. You're too stunning to let an opportunity to have you in my arms pass. I'll seek out these other available ladies after our dance, shall I?"

A breath I didn't realize I'd been holding leaves my lungs with a sigh of relief. "Sounds good to me." I grin and then he's gone—

Weston's pulled him away from me and now stands between us. "Hands off. She's spoken for." He glares at Chad.

"Weston," I try, but he turns his glare on me then turns around completely to face me.

"Fuck this, Tory. I'm done waiting. I told Finn about us. It's done." Then, his lips are on mine in a savagely possessive kiss, devouring any protest I might have.

Weston

Ten Minutes Ago . . .

I can handle waiting another two weeks to be with Tory. I can. If I keep telling myself that, I'll believe it eventually. And it isn't just the physical aspect of our relationship that I want to begin already. I want to be able to come home from work and kiss her. I want to hold her hand or tug her into my lap when we hang out with our friends.

If I've learned anything in the last couple of months, it's that life is fleeting. And I don't want to waste any more time. But Tory needs to do this on her own terms, and if all I have to do is wait two little weeks to make her happy, then I will.

I'd been a dick earlier, and I feel like shit for it. I shouldn't have taken it out on her. I know she wants to be with me.

Holding her in my arms now, in this goddamn dress, with her breasts pushed up against my chest, I'm struggling not to drag her off this dancefloor and shove her into a supply closet so I can worship her amazing body. That or wrap her up in my jacket so the other dudes in the room stop ogling her.

Someone is going to end up with a broken nose if I don't get my shit together.

Then, out of the blue, someone taps my shoulder. Shifting my gaze, there's a middle-aged guy standing there, eyeing Tory like she's a tender, juicy steak. I grit my teeth. I really want to ignore him, but then he speaks.

"May I cut in?" he asks.

Tory looks at him and frowns. "I'm sorry, what's your name?"

I stand there, dumbfounded, as Tory runs her eyes over his entire body, and the fucker grins at my woman. Then, he holds his hand out to her, waiting for her to shake it. She gives me the side-eye before reaching out and placing her palm in his, then he introduces himself.

"I'm Nixie's single, baggage-free uncle, Chad." His eyes eat her up. And I want to wipe that smug-ass grin off his face.

Tory releases a startled laugh. "Ah, nice to meet you, Chad. I assume you know who I am since you're the one trying to cut in on my best man time." She gestures to me with her chin.

I still have one hand curled around her, and my fingers tense at Chad's mention of being single. Tory notices and subtly moves her hand down to hold mine.

Chad smirks. "I believe I'm supposed to be *your* designated wedding sex."

My entire body tenses. I clench my fist as rage and jealousy fill me. How fucking dare he? And why the fuck is it okay for him to speak to her like that? It really fucking isn't. But before I can drop him, Tory rotates her body into mine, bringing herself between us.

"Can you give me a minute?" she asks *me*—fucking *me*. She wants *me* to give *her* a minute with her designated wedding sex. I don't fucking think so. She gets up on her tiptoes and moves slightly closer to me and whispers, "Let me get to the bottom of this, then I'll come find you."

No fucking way is she handling this on her own. I glare

at him over her exposed shoulder. He knows the score, and he doesn't care. What a piece of shit. He knows we are a couple. I can see it in his twisted smirk.

I'm handling this. Now.

Giving Tory a curt nod, I turn on my heel and push my way through the throng of dancers around us until I spot Finn and Nixie getting cozy in the far corner of the restaurant.

I storm over to them, not caring who gets in my way. They soon move when they see me coming anyway. As soon as I reach my target, I lay it all out. "I'm in love with Tory. She's terrified she'll lose you if she's with me, but you wouldn't do that to her, now would you?" It is a demand, not a question, and the taut expression on his face tells me he knows it too.

Nixie grins. "Chad introduced himself, did he?" She bats her lashes innocently.

My glare shifts to her. "You—what the fuck, Nix? You set this up?"

She grins wider, and looking all proud of herself, she announces, "Yep."

Now, she has not only my glare fixed on her, but Finn's too. "What the fuck? What's going on here?" Finn demands of his new wife.

Turning into him, she looks up at him from beneath her lashes. "It's clear as day how they feel about each other. The only person who can't see it baby, is you. I'm sorry, but they're suffering because they're both afraid of losing you. I won't let that happen. We're a family, the four of us. And they're hurting having to stay away from each other.

"Remember what that was like, Finn? When I was too afraid to be with you? It hurt both of us. I don't want that for them, and neither do you," she says as she gazes at him with love and compassion in her eyes.

It makes so much sense when she puts it like that. Why hadn't I thought to put it to him like that? Right, because I'm not a chick.

Finn's expression softens as she speaks. And damn it, so does mine. I want to be mad at her for fucking with us like that, but she did it with good intentions. I can't hold that against her.

I watch my best friend as he processes everything his wife said, and I wait for him to respond. It feels like forever before he finally looks at me. "If this is some sick MILF thing, you'll be dead to me. Got it? There won't be a second chance if you fuck this up."

My eyes widen. "You know it's not like that. It never has been."

He closes his eyes and shakes his head. "I don't know what to think right now. Because, apparently, my mom and best friend have been jonesing for each other, and I thought you were just being the man-whore extraordinaire you have always been around her."

I grimace and shake my head. "It's never been like that with her, Finn. I joked about it to make it seem that way." I rub the back of my neck. "I guess I wanted you to think I was just dicking around. I mean, it's not like I could tell you I had fallen for your mom."

Finn cringes. "I think I preferred it when I thought you were just being a dick."

I nod. "Yeah, I know. But we're still cool, though, right?"

Finn looks between me, Nixie, and then over to the dance floor where Chad still has his hands all over my woman, then back to me. "I'll get over it—eventually." He grins and mock-punches me in the shoulder.

That's my cue. I don't waste any more time as I hot-foot it back to Tory. As soon as I'm close enough, I reach out and yank Chad's shoulder, pulling him away from Tory. "Hands off. She's spoken for." I can't stop glaring at the guy, even though I know Nix put him up to it.

"Weston," Tory whispers from behind me.

I turn around fully so I can look at her. I'm still glaring. I'm so worked up at this point I can't stop. And my words come out harsher than I mean. "Fuck this, Tory. I'm done waiting. I told Finn about us. It's done."

Before she can protest, I drop my head to her level and kiss her in front of everyone. Voices hush around us as I get lost in the feel of her lips against mine. I can't stop, so I deepen the kiss, sliding my tongue across her plump bottom lip.

Finally, her hands move from her sides and up to hold my biceps. Then, they slowly glide up over my shoulders, my neck, and into my hair at my nape. I fucking love it when she does that.

My hands squeeze her hips tighter as I draw her body in closer so I can feel all her lush curves against me. I groan into her mouth and—

Someone taps my shoulder.

Reluctantly, I pull back and glance over my shoulder at the offending hand still placed there.

Finn is standing behind me, looking none too impressed. "When I said I'd get over it, I meant it, but it would be a lot easier to do if I didn't have to witness you dry humping my mom on the dance floor at my wedding—or ever, actually."

I grin. "I'll try to control myself." I wink, and he shakes his head.

Poking his head around my shoulder, he smiles at a furiously blushing Tory. "Hey," he says, "it's time for the father-daughter dance. I was thinkin' you and I could take a spin around the floor and show 'em how it's really done."

Tory releases a sigh of relief and steps away from me and into Finn's waiting arms.

Chapter Twenty-Two

Victoria

THIS MOMENT, RIGHT HERE, IS THE HAPPIEST MOMENT OF MY life.

Dancing with my son at his wedding after the man of my dreams claimed me as his in front of everyone we know. I don't think I'll ever stop smiling.

"You love him, don't you?" Finn asks me.

He doesn't seem mad or upset. And I am *so* relieved. "Yeah, I think I do," I answer honestly.

Finn nods as we twirl around the floor, making rings around Nixie and her father. "Okay, I'll deal then. But if you could keep the lip locking to a minimum around me, that'd be great," he says, smiling.

After Vera had given us her blessing, it lifted a huge weight off my shoulders. But having Finn be okay with it... I don't have words for how amazing I feel right now. "I'll see what I can do," I murmur, grinning.

Finn rolls his eyes. "Gee, thanks for being so considerate after I'm being so gracious as to give you the go ahead to start—wait, what were the words you used that day you found me and Nix on the living room couch?" He scrunches up his face as he tries to remember. "Got it! Bumping uglies. So, I've just given you the okay so start bumping uglies with my best friend, and all you can say is, 'I'll see what I can do'?" he mimics my voice, and I have to laugh.

"I do not sound like that. And fine, I'll keep him on a tight leash when we're all together, better?" I ask, still laughing.

"Eww, I don't need to know what kinky shit you two are into," he huffs. "But, if you could keep him contained, it would be appreciated."

One more round of the dance floor and the song comes to an end, and Weston is there, waiting to take me back into his arms.

"A little eager, are we?" I tease.

"Fuck yes. There's nothing keeping me away from you now." There is a wicked glint in his eyes, and my insides heat. "Now everyone knows you're mine," he says then closes the distance between our mouths and presses his lips to mine.

I don't think I'll ever get sick of Weston's kisses. Every single time his lips touch mine, I feel it throughout my whole body. I get lost in his touch, in the small sounds of approval he makes when I play with the hair at his nape, in the slide of his tongue against mine.

His lips travel to my ear. "Can we leave now? Please?" he murmurs against my neck.

A shiver races through me at the intention behind his words. Instead of answering him, I pull away and take his hand in mine, leading him off the dance floor. His cheeky smile and devilish gleam in his eyes tells me he has plans for me, and I am going to enjoy every moment of it.

I school my features as we approach Finn and Nixie. "Hey, guys, we're uh..." I give Weston the side-eye—you know the one, the one that says *There's no way they don't know we're leaving to have sex.* He just lifts a brow in response then shrugs.

Clearing my throat, I decide to throw caution to the wind. "So we're leaving so we can get busy already. Have a great honeymoon. Be safe, and text me when you get there." I go in for a quick hug and kiss on the cheek for each of them, and to say it's not awkward AF hugging Finn after telling him I am leaving to have sex with his friend would be a big fat lie.

But Nixie squeezes me tight and whispers in my ear, "I'm so glad Chad's wife couldn't make it. I never did like her anyway." She is grinning like a mad thing when we separate.

I gasp. "What?"

She shrugs. "If I was sick of waiting for you two to finally get it on, I know it must have been killing you," she laughs.

I shake my head. "You're a twisted little thing, Nix, but God I love you." I plaster one more quick kiss on her cheek as Weston begins tugging me toward the exit.

We pass Luke and Beth making out in the shadowed hallway on our way out, and Weston pauses to yell out, "Night, Lukey. Don't be a fool, wrap your tool, bro."

Luke's head shoots up, embarrassment coating his cheeks, and Beth drops her head and looks at the ground like it is the most interesting thing since sliced bread. When Luke notices Weston's hand wrapped around my waist, he grins. "Finally, dude! Took you long enough to grow a pair."

Weston scoffs but doesn't reply. I wave from beside him, then he continues dragging me out the door. Once outside, he lets our driver know we're ready, and the car is brought around.

My body zings with nervous excitement. I can't wait to be alone with him, yet at the same timc, I'm a little apprehensive. There's no going back from here. But as I gaze up at his shadowed profile beside me, I know I don't want to go back.

I want every single thing that's about to happen and everything after.

EXCITED ENERGY FLOODS MY SYSTEM AS WE SIT QUIETLY IN THE backseat of the town car that has driven us around all day. Tory's hand on my thigh keeps me steady, keeps me grounded. But internally, I am at war with myself.

Finally, after all these years, Tory and I will be together. In every sense of the word.

And I can't decide if I want to take my time with her, savor her, and explore every little inch of her body, or if I want to rip her dress off as soon as we walk in the door, press her up against the wall, and take her right there.

My cock springs to life as I mull over my next move.

Tory's hand slides to the inside of my thigh and up, up, up, until she's stroking my cock through my suit pants. I want to take them off, feel her delicate fingers wrapped around my bare flesh. But not yet. I have to wait until we are at least inside the house before clothes start coming off.

Cool it, Wes. You've got all night and every night after that. Just chill.

My jaw clenches as she begins to apply more pressure with her palm and increases her pace. My hips move with her, encouraging her exploration. I reach around and grip the side of her face, bringing it to me so I can ravage her mouth while she strokes me.

The kiss is rough, messy, hot. My fingers tangle in her hair. "Fuuck, Tor. I've waited so long for this."

"Me too," she pants just as the car slows to a halt outside

her house. Well, it has kinda become my house, too, recently.

Our house. I like the sound of that.

I open the door, climb out, then extend my hand for Tory. She takes it as she slides over and out. I thump on the top of the car twice after closing the door to let the driver know he can take off.

Tory rummages through that tiny thing she calls a purse for her key as I stand close behind her, my hands massaging her hips. She presses her ass back into me, and I groan at the feel of her full cheeks pressed against my cock. "Hurry up, Tory, or I'm going to fuck you on the front porch for the whole street to see."

Her body shudders at my words, and she finally gets the key in the lock and swings the door open. We practically fall inside, and I slam the door shut behind me. Before I can even take a step forward, Tory is on me, hands in my hair, clawing at me as she pulls my mouth down to hers.

My hands go to the back of her dress, and I tug at the laces until they come loose. She wiggles a little and the dress falls to the floor leaving her standing before me in her pink-and-cream heels, a pink lace thong, and a sticky thing stuck to her boobs.

I tilt my head to the side; it looks like chicken fillets have been glued to her chest. I'm about to ask what it is when she starts to peel it off.

"Stick-on bra," she explains, clearly having read my expression.

"Never seen one of those before," I murmur, my gaze fixed on her perfect tits. So round, so full. They swing just a little from their weight, and a pulse shoots through my dick at the thought of one day fucking them.

While I stand there, staring, she hooks her thumbs into the sides of her thong and slowly drags it down her toned thighs. I follow every movement with my eyes until she kicks it to the side. Then, I trace the long line of her legs back up to the place ninety percent of my fantasies have taken place.

I drop to my knees. She is breathtaking. Absolutely stunning. Nothing in my fantasies has been nearly as good as the real thing. She stands proud before me, in all her naked glory, and I want to worship her body for the rest of my life.

Placing, first, one soft kiss on her stomach, my mouth travels to her hip, down her thigh, over her mound to the opposite thigh. Her legs tremble as I make my way back closer to her pussy again. "Who's eager now?" I tease.

"Shut up and stop teasing me," she groans in frustration, and I fucking love it.

"Yes, ma'am," I say right before sliding my tongue between her pussy lips, separating them so I can get to her clit. I steady her with one hand, wrap my other around her ankle and hook it over my shoulder. A shuddering whimper breaches her lips and I reach around behind her, digging my fingers into her full ass cheek, pulling her pussy toward my face. I suck her little bundle of nerves into my mouth and stroke it with my tongue until she begs me to stop.

"Weston, I can't, stop, I'm, oh God." The words fall from her lips, and I reluctantly pull away.

Gripping the backs of her thighs and her ass, I look up at her. She is the most beautiful thing I've ever seen. Her chest heaves as she struggles to catch her breath, yet the biggest smile I've ever seen curves her lips. She tugs on my hair. "You. Bedroom. Now."

I lower her leg and am on my feet in seconds, sweeping

her off hers in another. She lets out a surprised yelp and clings to my shoulders as I stride down the hallway to our room. I kick the door open and drop her on the bed.

My eyes eat her up, splayed out for me in nothing but those heels. My cock aches to get closer to her, to feel her smooth skin against my mine.

She licks her lips as she eyes me. "Clothes off," she commands, and who am I to refuse?

I strip in record time, popping a few buttons on the new dress shirt I'd bought for the wedding, and I don't give a flying fuck. As soon as the last sock is gone, I am on her.

Pinning her hands to the bed on either side of her head, I take my time getting to know her tits, licking and nibbling as I explore. Tory's back arches, pushing her breasts further into my face as I suck a nipple into my mouth. She starts thrashing and moaning, so I suck harder. Then, I release one of her wrists so I can feel just how wet I know she is for me.

My finger slides between her soaked folds to her entrance. I trace around it gently while I suck her nipple harder, then I slam my finger inside her, massaging her G-spot. A piercing cry leaves Tory's lips as she arches higher and begins to shudder beneath me.

I let her nipple pop from my mouth and continue to gently slide my finger in and out of her as she rides out her orgasm.

Panting, she takes my face in her hands and pulls me down to kiss her. Long languid strokes of our tongues, soft nibbles of lips, a slow build back to ravenous.

"Condoms are in the side table drawer," Tory whispers. "Get one for me, I want to put it on you."

I nod and quickly shift to shuffle through the drawer. Not being able to find one fast enough, I flick on the table lamp to help me see. She has a whole box in there. "Planning to have a party?" I ask as I fish one out and hand it to her.

She's sitting up now, her knees folded beneath her. I swallow at the sight of her. God, I love her. I love everything about her. She takes my breath away every single day. I wonder if a day will come when her effect on me isn't as potent, but I doubt it.

I watch as she rips open the small foil packet with her teeth and pulls the condom from the wrapper. I stay standing at the very edge of the bed, and she shuffles forward to reach me. Her breasts sway with every move she makes, and I swear, I get harder.

Tory looks up at me before wrapping her hand around my length and squeezing gently. "I love the feel of your cock," she breathes. "So smooth, so hard. I want to taste it." Then she drops her head and sucks the tip into her warm mouth, and I almost come on the spot.

"Fuuuck," I grit as she increases her suction and slides her hand up and down my shaft.

All too soon, she releases my dick with a pop. When she peers up into my eyes, hers are glazed, almost feral with lust. I swallow hard. "You better hurry up with that condom, Victoria, or I'm going to fuck you without it. Consequences be damned."

Her eyes light up, but she does as I ask and slides the condom over my dick. As soon as it is on, I push her back down on the bed, spread her legs, and crawl up her body. She can't stay still beneath me, her body as wired as mine.

I shudder as my cock breaches her entrance. How long have I waited for this day?

Tory squirms, then her hands are on my ass, urging me to push further, harder, deeper. So I do. Inch by inch, I thrust my hips in and out of her, going a little deeper each time. She feels amazing. She feels right.

"Jesus, Tory, you're so perfect," I groan against her throat.

"Weston," she says. "Fuck me like you fantasized about when you were seventeen."

I can't refuse her, and truth be told, I've been fantasizing about this moment since well before I turned seventeen. But it wasn't until then that I'd actually begun to see her as more than my best friend's hot as fuck mom. I wanted to know her intimately, and now I do.

Sliding out then back in slowly, I push up onto my forearms. "Are you sure? I was a kinky little fucker."

She licks her lips, excitement shining in her eyes, and she nods eagerly.

I pull all the way out and quickly flip her over, grab her hips, and drag them up just a little before slapping her ass. Then I slam back inside her. "Oh, God!" she cries out as I thrust into her relentlessly. My fingertips sink into one of her hips, the other hand gripping the back of her neck, as I hold her in place. Her hands shoot out and grip the edge of the mattress as I fuck her with everything I have.

"That's right Tor, look at you taking my dick like such a good girl," I pant on a roll of my hips. "I knew you'd look amazing with my cock buried deep inside this pretty pussy."

She whimpers, pushing back into me. "Yes Wes, yes, more," she begs.

My hand rears back, then connects with her ass again in a sharp slap making her arch her hips up higher. I smooth my palm over the sting, then bring my hand to my lips and suck my thumb until it's dripping wet.

The tight pucker of her asshole taunts me every time she

pushes back onto my dick, and I trace around the sensitive hole with my slippery thumb.

She quivers under my touch, her face turning to peer at me over her shoulder, then nods.

Before she can second guess it, I push the tip of my thumb inside her at the same time I slide my cock into her pussy. A keening cry rips from her lips and she clenches around me as she pushes her face into the comforter and screams. The tight walls of her pussy pulse around my shaft, and that's all I can take.

I follow her over the edge into the most powerful orgasm I've ever had.

Chapter Twenty-Three

Victoria

I AWAKE TO ROUGH FINGERS TRAILING DOWN MY SPINE, AND I shiver.

"Morning," Weston's husky voice whispers against my neck as he bends down and brushes soft kisses along my throat, across my chin to my mouth. I kiss him back as his tongue slides between my lips.

A contented sigh slides past my lips. "Morning," I whisper back, almost afraid if I speak normally, I'll ruin the peacefulness surrounding us.

His grin is panty melting—if I were wearing any, that is.

Reaching up, I run my fingers through his shaggy hair, scratching my nails over his scalp the way I'd learned last night that he very much enjoys. He nips at my jaw playfully, and I smile. I could wake up like this every day.

Weston props himself on an elbow, resting his head in his palm. "So, what are we going to do today?" he asks while tracing patterns on my stomach with his free hand.

I roll toward him. "I thought we were doing it?" I say with

a little wink then start laughing at the expression that comes over his face. "What?" I ask.

His eyes fix on my breasts, his breathing becomes heavy, and he licks his lips. I swear I can feel that small swipe of his tongue all the way down to the tips of my toes. "Wes?" I murmur.

He blinks but doesn't shift his focus from the girls. "My eyes are up here," I chuckle softly.

Breathing heavily through his nose, he says, "I've been looking into those beautiful eyes for years. And while I'll never get sick of them, I'm busy right now."

I laugh and grab the sheet to pull it up and cover myself, only for him to slap my hands away. "What are you doing?" he demands.

"Removing the distraction," I say.

"Fuck that." He shoots out, and in one fluid movement, rolls me to my back and straddles me. "I've got a lot of lost time to make up for. I'm going to spend all day worshiping this body."

I swallow. "Uh, okay. I think I can handle that," I mumble. But I'm not entirely sure I can. If I am completely honest, my previously neglected vagina is a wee bit tender today. My vibrator did nothing to prepare me for the size of Weston's cock, which is currently sitting up against his ripped stomach.

Maybe I can handle just a little more...

NOTHING HAS EVER BEEN AS PERFECT AS TORY SPLAYED OUT beneath me.

Her full tits lay heavy on her chest, begging to be played with. But the curve of her thighs call to me too. I want to run my hands over every inch of her.

While she was sleeping this morning, I discovered a freckle beneath her left ass cheek. It is the cutest thing I've ever seen. I want to lick that freckle. "By the way, I've named the freckle below your left ass cheek," I say as my hands skate around the curve of her tits and down her sides.

She is breathing heavily. "What freckle?"

I lift onto my knees, wrap my hands around her hips, and flip her onto her stomach. Then, I move down her legs until I'm sitting on her calves. "This one," I say, leaning down to kiss it.

"Oh," she breathes. "What's its name?"

"Bonita," I murmur as I slide my tongue over the spot.

"Uh-huh," Tory groans.

"It means pretty in Spanish. Did you know I took Spanish in high school? Aced it, too. That means I can whisper dirty things to you while I fuck you, and you'll think I'm whispering sweet nothings."

Unconsciously, she pushes her ass up and back toward me. My palm glides over the plump globes, and I can't resist; I lift my hand then bring my palm down in a swift slap to her cheek. She cries out and quivers under my touch.

If I weren't already turned on from lying in bed with a naked Tory, I sure as fuck am now after her reaction. "I hope you don't have plans today, because if I have my way, we won't be leaving this room," I tell her, and I mean it.

THE REST OF THE WEEKEND IS A BIT OF A BLUR. I CAN'T GET enough of Tory, and thankfully, she can't get enough of me.

When I have to leave for work on Monday morning, I drag my feet as I head for the door. Tory just rolls her eyes. "Oh, poor baby, too tired to go to work," she coos with a mock pout.

"You wore me out, woman!" I accuse. "This is your fault. How am I supposed to build houses when you've bled me dry of my life force?"

She cracks up laughing. "Oh, okay, I guess I better keep my hands to myself during the week then? Can't have you slacking."

Reaching for her, I pull her into my arms. "No need to be so dramatic, Tor. I'll think of something, don't you worry your pretty little head about it." Dropping one final kiss on her lips, I walk out the door and get in my truck.

Driving to the worksite, I think about how much things have changed in such a short time. It is only October and already so much has happened.

Finn and Nix got married. Tory quit her job and started her own business. I took over the small construction company I started working for as a teenager—not that I've mentioned that to Tory yet. I'll have to tell her soon.

I had planned on telling her, but then Mom died, and everything went to hell.

My chest tightens when I think about my mom, especially that she's not here to see Tory and me finally together. She would be so happy for us. Through every turn, she was always my biggest supporter.

When this year started, I'd been ready to give up on Tory ever seeing me as more than Finn's best friend. But Mom was the one who told me to hold out a little longer. I don't know how she knew it would work out between us, but somehow, she did.

I don't know what would have happened if I didn't have Tory through losing Mom. Having her close was enough to help ease the constricting weight from my chest enough that I could breathe. But she has done so much more than that for me. She helped me heal.

A day will never go by that I won't miss my mom. But Tory's shown me that I'll always have her in my heart. And I do. I feel her with me even now. She is happy for me, for us.

The only thing that could possibly make me happier in this moment, would be my ring on Tory's finger. If I didn't think she'd freak the fuck out, I'd go pick one up right now. But I know my woman, and she would lose her shit if I came home with an engagement ring. So that will just have to wait —for now.

As I pull into the site, my phone chimes with a text from her.

TORY: Can you be home by 5? I've got a surprise for you.

Grinning like a fool, I flick a quick text back.

WESTON: I'll talk to the boss, but I'm sure it'll be fine.

I decide I'll tell her about the company after whatever her surprise is.

Victoria

I CAN'T WAIT FOR WESTON TO GET HOME. I KNOW HE'S GOING to love my surprise. I've been so wired today that I've finished three new pieces and started the design for another. My body hums with excitement.

As soon as he gets home, I push him into the bathroom. "Shower, quickly. We've gotta be there in twenty minutes."

He looks back at me over his shoulder as he pulls his shirt over his head. "Where are we going?" he asks then undoes his belt buckle and slowly drags it through the belt loops. "Tory? Babe? Where are we going?" he asks again with a cocky smirk.

I blink a few times. I will never get sick of looking at him. He is so damn fine. My mouth waters as he steps out of his dirty jeans and into the shower, running his hands through his hair as the water pours over his sculpted body. "Uh, what?"

He chuckles and repeats himself, "Where are we going?"

"Oh, umm, it's a surprise," I say as my eyes eat him up.

His hand slides down his abs, along that magical V, and down to his hard shaft. I swallow as he leisurely pumps his fist around it.

"Do we have time for you to join me?" he asks, his voice deep and carnal.

"Uh..." I lick my lips. "No, no, I shouldn't. We'll be late."

He grins. "Suit yourself." Then, he turns his back on me,

bracing one hand on the tiles above his head as he continues to stoke himself.

God damn it, that ass is amazing. But I can't—I mean, I shouldn't.

We don't have time.

I glance at my watch; the appointment isn't until six . . . and it is only five-fifteen. Screw it, we can be quick.

Stripping off in record time, I climb into the shower behind Weston and wrap my arms around him, knocking his hand away from my prize. I grip his thick shaft in one hand and glide the other up over his defined abdominal muscles.

God, he feels good under my palms. His skin is so smooth I want to lick every inch of him. But we don't have time, I remind myself. Getting up on my tippy toes, I bite down on his shoulder. "We have to be quick," I murmur against his wet flesh.

A shiver runs down his spine and right through me before he spins around and pins me against the opposite wall. "I can do quick," he says right as his mouth meets mine in a deep, drugging kiss.

My back arches, and my body aches to get closer to him. He knows exactly what I want and lifts one of my thighs, wrapping it around his waist. "Hold on, Tor, this isn't going to be gentle."

I shudder violently at his words; I'm more than ready for him. I lift myself as high as I can on my tiptoes as he positions himself at my entrance. As soon as he nudges the head inside of me, he lifts my other leg and wraps it around his back too. I lock my ankles behind him, bringing myself closer still and pulling Weston's cock all the way inside.

His face drops to my neck as he sucks on my throat and pumps his hips furiously. It doesn't take long before my body tightens around him. I can't get enough, but I need—"More," I moan.

Weston's hands grip my hips so tightly I know he will leave bruises. His fingers dig deeper as he pounds harder. My orgasm rushes through me, and I throw my head back against the wall and groan as my body quivers uncontrollably.

Weston pulls out as soon as my orgasm subsides and comes against my stomach.

I grin at him dreamily. I've never been happier.

We wash quickly after our impromptu shower sex.

"What should I wear?" Weston asks as he moves things around in the drawer I'd cleared out for him a few weeks back.

"Shorts and a tee will be fine," I tell him as I grab the clothes I'd had on before my second shower of the day. I'd only just showered an hour before he got home.

Fifteen minutes later, I park my car in front of The Parlor and grin at Weston.

His eyes flick from the shop front, to me, then back again. "Are we getting tattoos?"

I nod. "Yep."

We walk in hand in hand and tell the receptionist we have an appointment. She lets us know Talia will be out in a few minutes, and we take a seat in the waiting area.

"So, what are we getting?" Weston asks.

I pull out my phone and show him the quote I'd sent in when I made the appointment. "Remember when you told me your heart beats for me?" I ask as he looks at the words on the screen. "Well, I haven't been able to get you out of my head since that day."

He nods, and slowly, his eyes raise to meet mine, shining

with so much emotion my breath catches in my throat. "It's perfect," he whispers then leans over and kisses me so tenderly, I swoon toward him when he eventually draws back.

The first sentence is for me. The second, for him.

"Always on my mind... Forever in my heart."

Chapter Twenty-Four

Weston

Six Months Later . . .

For the last six months, I've been hanging out on cloud nine. It is my first visit to the clouds, and I like it.

Our relationship has progressed faster than most, since I was kind of already living with her when we got together; I just never moved out. We've fallen into a natural rhythm, and everything between us seems so effortless now. I put it down to it having taken so long for us to figure our shit out and get together in the first place.

We had so many things to overcome before we could even be together. Finn, our age difference, my mom, then losing her. It was all so much, and now, it's smooth sailing.

Finn's gotten used to seeing us as a couple, and that makes a huge difference. I don't give a fuck what anyone else thinks; his opinion was the only one that ever mattered to me. But Tory had other concerns in addition to Finn's feelings.

She was too worried about other people's thoughts and perceptions. Initially, she'd been edgy when we'd go out together and people we knew saw us. She'd get nervous and start picking at her nails.

It only took it happening a couple of times before I had enough. After that, whenever it happened, I'd throw my arm around her shoulders, tug her into my side and tell them that we were a couple, and if they had any issue with it, they could kindly fuck off.

Nine times out of ten, people didn't care, and the remainder were inconsequential.

It didn't take long for Finn and me to fall back into our old pattern, which I'm eternally grateful for. I mean, he had every right to be pissed—I'm banging his mom.

But he got over it fairly fast, and I'm pretty sure Nix played a big role in making that happen.

Our little group of four expanded to six, now including Luke and Beth on a regular basis. They've been hooking up casually since the wedding, and Luke's only recently stepped it up and told her he wants exclusive rights. Not the finest word choice, but it worked for him. They've been an official couple for a couple of months now.

I couldn't be happier with where my life is headed. I have the woman of my dreams on my arm and in my bed. My best friend is happily married to the coolest nerd I've ever known. And our circle of friends has grown.

The only thing missing is my mom.

I know wherever she is, she's happy for us. She never told me my feelings for Tory were stupid, and she never minimized them either. I don't know how, but she always believed we would get together someday. And her faith in that was what kept me going when I thought Tory would never be able to get over the things keeping us apart.

And as always, Mom was right.

Now, I have the girl.

I have everything.

Victoria

Another Six Months Later . . .

Pulling my head out of the toilet, I flop onto the bathroom floor. This is getting old real fast. I've become very well acquainted with the toilet bowl in recent weeks. Weston is bouncing off the walls excited. Me, not so much.

I never expected this.

So, it was a shock when I found out.

I refuse say it's an accident because, quite frankly, I hate it when people refer to their children as mistakes or accidents. It's cruel and demeaning.

No, this baby is no accident. Weston and I have sex—and a lot of it. He is insatiable... but I'm not much better. Even now, curled around the base of the toilet, I can see him getting out of bed to come check on me, his abs rippling as he sits up. And his forearms… oh God, his forearms. A dreamy sigh escapes me as he enters the bathroom.

He kneels beside me. "Hey, you," he murmurs as he sweeps my bangs from my eyes. "You done? Wanna come back to bed?" he asks gently.

I take a deep breath and think about it. My stomach has settled, and the spinning in my head has stopped. "Let me brush my teeth first," I tell him as I rearrange myself into a sitting position.

He stands, gets my toothbrush, puts just the right amount of toothpaste on it, and then wets it under the tap before handing it to me. "Here you go, Momma," he says with a cheeky grin.

A pathetic half laugh leaves my lips as I take the toothbrush from him and begin scrubbing my nasty mouth while sitting on the floor.

Weston sits on the edge of the bathtub and waits for me to finish. When I'm done, I hand it back to him, and he, in turn, hands me a glass of water. I swish it around inside my mouth then spit it back into the empty cup and hand it back to him.

He rinses them in the sink then sets them to dry on the counter before bending down to pick me up. We have this whole thing down to a fine art.

Carrying me over to my side of the bed, he sets me down gently against the headboard then pulls the blanket back up and sits on the edge beside me. Toying with my fingers, he asks, "So, you ready to talk to Finn yet?"

I know it's coming, and I know it is unavoidable.

But the question remains—*How do you tell your son, you're having his best friend's baby?*

BONUS SCENE—YOU'RE GOING TO BE A BIG BROTHER

MOM AND WES ARE NOWHERE IN SIGHT WHEN NIX AND I arrive at the newest cafe in Shiloh Springs, Perky's Books & Brews. It's surprisingly busy so we snag a table near the front window as group get up to leave.

I shoot off a text to Wes letting him know we're here, and he replies a few minutes later.

WESTON: Sorry dude, we'll be there in fifteen. Tor wasn't feeling well this morning.

Worry tightens my gut. I haven't seen her in a couple of weeks, which is weird in itself. We usually have dinner once a week as a family, but she's begged off the last two times, saying she wasn't feeling well.

Is she sick? Like, sick, sick?

"Fuck," I mutter under my breath, running my free hand through my hair.

Nixie frowns, and takes my cell from me. "Finn, what's wrong? You've gone pale." Her eyes flit over the texts, and she frowns harder as she looks to me. "Finn?"

Meeting Nix's concerned gaze, I swallow past the lump in my throat. "Do you think something's wrong with her?"

She tilts her head. "Like what?"

"Like, I don't know. Something bad. She canceled family dinner the last couple of weeks, and now they're late because she wasn't feeling well..."

Nix takes my hand and laces our fingers together. "Tory wouldn't keep something like that from you baby. You know that."

Do I know that, though?

I want Nixie's words to comfort me, I really do. But... I shake my head. "She was in love with my best friend for how long before she told me, because she was worried about how I'd feel. If she was sick—"

"Hey, sorry we're late. My fault," Mom says, dropping down into the seat next to Nix.

Weston drags the chair beside me out from the table and sits. He elbows me in the ribs with a snort. "Well it certainly doesn't take us half an hour just to brush our hair."

It has never taken mom that long to get ready to go out. She's just not one of those women. But as I look at her closer, I can tell she's wearing make-up.

That's it, something's up, I can feel it. "Is it cancer?" I ask, cutting straight through the bullshit and getting right to the point.

Everyone gapes at me and I toss my hands in the air. "Don't act like nothing is wrong. I know you're keeping something from me, you're wearing make-up for fuck sake." I narrow my eyes at my mom, then my supposed best friend.

"Wha—cancer?" Mom says at the same time as Weston announces, "We're pregnant!"

Now it's my turn to gape. I'm struck silent.

My wife however, is not. She throws her arms around mom's shoulders as a million questions pour from her lips.

"How far? Boy or girl? Do you have any names yet? When are you due?—"

Nix is still talking when Wes's words finally sink in. A baby. *My mom* and *my best friend*, are. Having. A. Baby.

What the fuck am I supposed to do with that? It only just stopped being weird seeing them being together. Now they're making babies.

My head throbs as I slowly turn in my seat until I'm fully facing Wes.

His eyes dart away from me, then back again. "What?"

"You knocked up my mom?" It's a legit struggle to force those words out because they create mental images I really don't want to see.

Wes swallows. "Ah, yeah. It would appear so."

I nod. Then nod again. That's when the silence around me penetrates. Nix, Mom, and Wes, are all staring at me. They're happy, tentative smiles on their faces, but they're holding them back. Because of me.

Weston clears his throat, drawing my attention back to him. He shrugs, then drops his hand on my shoulder, giving it a squeeze as a massive smile lights his face. "Congratulations man, you're going to be a big brother."

When he puts it like that, it hits different.

A big brother.

I'm going to be a big brother.

Gradually, the corner of my mouth curves up, and soon, I'm smiling too. Wes pulls me into a hug, slapping me on the back. "I knew you'd be cool with it. It's fucking exciting, right?"

Sitting back, I glare at him. "Yeah, not the words that initially came to mind. I was more thinking along the lines of *temporary insanity*."

He arches a brow. "Umm, what?"

"Temporary insanity," I repeat. "That was going to be my plea when I turned myself in for murdering my best friend for filling my head with horrific mental images of him and my mom making babies. You know I'll be spending the next year of my life attempting to scrub this shit from my brain. I only just rid of the last lot you put up in there, you bastard."

Wes grins, then says the same words he said to me when we were teenagers. "It's not my fault you've got a hot mom."

And just like I did back then, I slug him in the shoulder, hard. But this time, I'm smiling as I do it.

Epilogue

Victoria

Three Years Later . . .

"Finny!" C'elle squeals as she takes off running toward Finn and Nixie as they stroll up the drive hand in hand.

Finn swoops her up in his arms. "How's my favorite girl?" he asks as he tickles her ribs.

She giggles and wriggles under his hands. "Dop it, Finny."

He relents, only to start kissing her chubby little cheeks. "I've got a surprise for you, baby girl," he tells her as he moves her around to prop her on his hip.

C'elle turned two a couple of months ago, and Finn is her favorite person in the world. And apparently, the feeling is mutual. He's taken to being a big brother better than I could have hoped.

I thought he might feel weird about it. You know, with his best friend being his little sister's dad. But by the time I'd had her, he was over any mixed feelings about it and showed up at the hospital with a tiny gray sweater with 'Little Sister' written on it and matching leggings.

It was adorable, and what she wore home from the hospital.

Finn carries C'elle inside while Nixie carries in a salad she made to go with dinner. Nix still isn't a great cook, but she makes great salads. I take the bowl from her and pop it in the fridge, pulling out a bottle of wine and holding it up in offering to her.

To my surprise, she shakes her head. "No thanks, not tonight."

I frown. "Are you sick?" I ask, half joking, half serious.

Nix just shrugs and reaches for a can of lemon squash instead.

I narrow my eyes on her, but before I can grill her further, Luke waltzes in with Beth on his arm. "Hey, guys," I call over Nixie's head.

Luke nods in our direction then detours out the back door to the patio where Weston and Finn are knocking back a few beers. Beth approaches us with a huge grin on her face. Then, she extends her left hand and squeals, "He finally proposed!"

Nixie and I take turns congratulating her and eyeing the impressive rock that now takes up residence on Beth's left ring finger. "That thing's huge," I say. "No wonder it took him so long to pop the question; he was saving for that ring."

Beth laughs and tells us how Luke had spirited her away to the lake at sunrise yesterday and popped the question as the sun rose.

"Damn, who knew Luke was so romantic?" Nix notes, and I have to agree.

When Weston proposed, I was in labor—not the most

romantic setting, I can tell you. But I'd said yes all the same. Then, I proceeded to make sure he knew he was going to spend the rest of his life making it up to my vagina for inseminating me and forcing me to push a ginormous baby out of my precious lady bits.

He'd laughed initially then sobered when he realized I was deadly serious.

I had said a lot of things during my labor with C'elle, including demanding he take me home for a cup of tea because I'd had enough for one day and I'd try again tomorrow. I also remembered that I'd forgotten to feed the cat that morning, so he better take me home to rectify the situation immediately. Then, he pointed out that we didn't own a cat.

He learned that day to never correct a woman on the cusp of pushing a baby out.

We'd been trying to decide on a middle name for the last couple of weeks but couldn't choose between Jacqueline and Vera. When I went into labor on Jacq's birthday, the decision was made for us, and C'elle Jacqueline Banks entered the world, carrying her aunt's beautiful curly blonde hair.

Just then, C'elle comes rushing back inside, straight up to Nix, and does the strangest thing. She lifts Nixie's shirt and starts trying to look through her belly button. Nix bursts out laughing. "What are you doing, Princess?"

"Finny said deirs a baby in deir. But I don't see it," she complains.

My eyes shoot up to Nixie's face; she's blushing furiously. "Umm, surprise?" she mumbles as I fly toward her, wrapping my arms around her.

"Oh my God! That's fantastic, how far along are you?" I ask.

"Twelve weeks." She grins.

Finn strolls in behind her and rests his arm around her shoulders. "Hey, Grandma," he teases, and my hand reacts before my brain does, flying out to smack him upside the head for calling me such an awful name.

But then I realize I am going to be a grandma. At the ripe old age of thirty-six, I will be a grandma. I suddenly have a feeling I know how Finn felt when I told him he was going to be a big brother at twenty-four.

"As ecstatically happy as I am for you right now, you are never to call me that again. We're going to have to come up with a suitable alternative," I tell him as I pull him in for a hug.

How far my life has come in just a few short years. And I wouldn't change any of it for the world.

THE END